UNDERCOVER MAGIC

DRAGON'S GIFT THE VALKYRIE BOOK 1

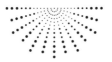

LINSEY HALL

To Ora and Richard Callaway, with all my love.

CHAPTER ONE

The *Real* Death Valley
California, USA

"Hurry!" I shouted. "The sun is almost up!"

The engine of our monster truck roared as my sister Ana, the driver, pressed on the gas and laughed like a loon. I grinned. The nut job loved speed. I crouched low on the platform built over the car's hood and clung to the railing, eyeing the terrain ahead for oncoming threats.

Daylight was the most dangerous time in Death Valley. That's when the monsters crept out. Normally night would be the most dangerous time, right? Well, not here. Even the sun was a weapon in the valley.

This was the time it really got dangerous.

We should have been home before daylight, but our last job transporting outlaws across the valley had run late, leaving us out here at the worst time of day.

Right now, to be precise.

While Ana drove the truck, it was my job to blast away any monsters that might want to snack on us.

I was a lot of things, but monster snack wasn't one of them.

"To the left, Bree!" my sister shouted.

I squinted into the distance. The weak morning sun painted the desert valley in shades of gray and gold. A salt monster hurtled toward us on sturdy legs made of slabs of pressed salt. We were driving through the Bad Water, a dried-out old salt lake, and these were the guardians. One hit with their giant hands could pulverize puny mortals like us.

"Ah, dang! These guys are the worst." Salt monsters were a witch to take out, even with my sonic boom power.

I called upon the magic within me.

Come on, don't fail me now.

My power wasn't exactly reliable lately, but out here in the desert, I didn't have to worry about property damage or zapping innocents. We were the only fools dumb enough and desperate enough to work out here.

Anyway, all I had to do was hit the salt monsters.

Easy peasy.

Ha. As if.

Ana hooted and laid on the gas. The burst of speed jerked me backward, but the climbing harness strapped around my waist and legs yanked and kept me in place.

The monster thundered toward us, footsteps shaking the ground. Chips of salt rained off as it ran. The beast was at least twenty feet tall, and half as broad.

If I could pulverize him properly, he'd coat the rims of a lot of margarita glasses.

Hmmm... Could we sell that? Not a bad thought for later. We needed the cash.

I swallowed hard, focusing on the magic within me. It was like a stubborn light that zipped around in my chest, waiting for me to catch it and hurl it outward.

"There's another!" Ana cried.

Shoot. Fifty meters behind the first monster, there was a second, even bigger one.

"Head straight for him!" I called. A direct path would increase my chance of success.

Ana veered left, tires kicking up dirt and rocks. The first monster was twenty meters away now, its craggy white face glowering. It had pits for eyes and no mouth. A face only a mother could love.

I called on my magic, gathering it up in a bundle. It thrashed inside me, almost a wild thing, and I launched it outward. The power exploded forth, plowing into the dirt ten feet to the left of the salt monster. Gravel sprayed up.

"Dang it!" I called on the magic again, flinging it outward. It was a little easier this time, and the power shot toward the beast.

It slammed into the creature's chest, blasting him into a million pieces. Salt rained down like snow, and we sailed through it.

When I got it right, I got it *right.*

The buggy zoomed away from the salt rain. Buggy was a weird name for such a hulking machine, but we liked the dichotomy.

I licked the salt off my lips, wishing it really *was* coating the rim of a margarita glass, and squinted toward the next monster.

"Get ready to dodge!" I called upon my magic once again. I could already tell this one was going to be tricky. My power was partially drained, and he was *big.*

The earth trembled with the monster's footsteps. It was only thirty feet away. No distance at all, with the buggy going this fast.

I threw my magic at him. It plowed into his leg, obliterating the limb. The beast crashed to the ground.

"Right!" I screamed.

Ana jerked the vehicle toward the right. I clung to the railing, sliding on the platform. We swerved around the salt monster, but the beast reached out with one long arm and swiped at the side of our buggy.

His massive hand destroyed the metal spikes on the side, bending them backward. Though they were coated with deadly Ravener poison, it didn't affect a creature like him. The shriek of tearing metal sliced at my heart. There went the side door panels.

I loved the buggy. But worse than that, we didn't have the money to fix the machine, and we *needed* this thing for work. For survival.

"Rat bastard!" Ana screamed. It was currently her favorite curse word.

But salt monster wasn't down yet.

"Just keep going!" Quickly, I unclipped my harness and climbed over the front windshield. The truck had no top, just two bench seats where people could sit—or fight from if necessary, hurling magic without the restriction of a roof to stop them.

I scrambled by Ana, leaping over one bench seat and then the next, climbing onto the back platform.

"Safety first!" Ana hollered.

"Yeah, yeah." I clipped off my harness because she had a point. If I fell out of this truck, we were both dead.

Me, because I'd be monster chow, and Ana because she'd come after me even if I was a lost cause.

Behind us, the salt monster clambered to his feet. Uh, make that foot, singular. I'd blasted off the other one. Not that he let it stop him. Nope, old salty was using his arms as legs now, like some kind of strange orangutan. He lumbered after us, picking up speed.

"Come and get it, salt face!" I shouted.

"That's the best you got?" Ana yelled back.

"You don't like salt face?"

"I'm gonna be frank. It was weak."

I scoffed and heaved a sonic boom at the monster. It exploded out of me, *much* bigger than I'd expected, blasting me backward.

The harness jerked me to a stop, and my back ached like hell. My magic had always been tricky and weird, but lately it'd been even worse—sometimes huge, sometimes not.

I scrambled upright, clinging to the back railing. The blast had plowed into the salt monster, obliterating him. No surprise—it had been so big that I really hadn't had to aim.

"You get him?" Ana asked.

"Yeah!" I turned around, wind whipping my dark hair back from my face.

The sun was fully up now, illuminating the valley around us. Sloping mountains on either side rose up toward the clear blue sky, and the heat was already pressing down, suffocating. It was August, and if we didn't get out of here soon, it'd be hard to tell the difference between us and beef jerky.

"Almost there." Ana turned the buggy toward the mountain slope nearest us.

I inspected our surroundings for more threats, but once she directed the buggy to climb the slope, I relaxed. The deadly part of the valley—the one that humans knew nothing about—was trapped between two parallel rows of mountains. Now that we were leaving that behind, I could finally start breathing normally again.

I unhooked my harness and climbed onto the bench seat next to Ana, collapsing into it with an exhausted sigh and pulling off my dust goggles. I propped my booted feet up on the dash as the truck bounced over the rocks and looked at Ana.

She grinned at me, lifting up her goggles to reveal tired green eyes. Her once blonde mohawk was now pulled back in a long ponytail, a style that made it easier to blend into a crowd. She changed it a lot, but lately, it'd been a more subtle style. Her brown leather pants and strappy brown leather top made her look like she was in *Mad Max*, but the outfit worked out here. I wore the same, unless I wasn't fighting. In which case it was plain jeans and a tee.

Blending was important, especially for us. We might be leaving the monsters of Death Valley behind, but danger waited for us all the same. We'd been lying low all our lives, hiding from an unidentified threat. Hell, even those we paid to protect us were now hunting us.

"Did they tip?" I asked, mentally calculating what we'd need to make this month's payment on our concealment charms.

"No." Ana scowled. "Stingy jerks."

"Damn." Asking for tips was a new thing, but the monthly cost on our concealment charms had been jacked up, so we'd put out a tip jar in the buggy. Considering that we charged thousands for a trip across the valley, it wasn't surprising that folks weren't willing to cough up a little extra. "Ricketts is going to be pissed if we can't pay."

"He's already pissed. We already gave him the money from this job, and it wasn't enough." Ana gunned the engine and swerved around a boulder.

"Well, he shouldn't have jacked up the price."

"He does it because he can."

I scowled. We were at his mercy, and he knew it. After years of paying on the installment plan, he'd realized how desperate we were to stay hidden. So he'd jacked up the price, sending his bone crackers after us when we couldn't pay.

But we *needed* that charm to hide us from whoever hunted us.

After they'd come for us when we were five, we'd spent most of our lives hiding—first with our mother, and then alone—but we'd never figured out who hunted us or why. However, they'd killed our mother and maybe even our sister, Rowan, so the threat was pretty danged clear.

My running theory was that they wanted us because we were Unknowns. We were the only supernaturals of an unknown species that I'd ever met. There were mages, vampires, shifters, fae, demons, and monsters of all varieties.

And then there was us—anomalies. Freaks. Unknowns.

Marked by a four-pointed star at the tops of our spines. Marks we kept hidden by magic.

In a world where all magic should be identifiable and controllable according to our government, the Order of the Magica, being an Unknown was dangerous. Our magic was often incredibly strong...and uncontrollable. Throughout history, Unknowns were often killed out of fear or manipulated by others for their own purposes.

That was *not* gonna be us.

So we laid low, paying for our concealment charms—when we could afford it—and living on the outskirts of society.

The buggy crested the top of the mountain ridge, and the view spread out in front of us.

It was glorious, as always, with the desert stretching far and wide. In the distance, our little town of Death Valley Junction sat like a forgotten remnant of the Old West. It was one of the few all-magic towns in the world, hidden from humans by a spell called The Great Peace. The spell kept the existence of supernaturals on the down-low and led humans away from any of our towns.

It was the place we'd ended up after our mother's murder when we were thirteen. It'd been home for the ten years since. But even that was starting to look iffy, what with Ricketts sending his bone crackers after us.

I leaned forward and squinted, searching for any sight of Ricketts's goons. We'd gotten a warning visit recently, which meant we could look forward to seeing more of them soon.

"See 'em?" Ana asked.

"Nope." Just the usual light foot traffic between the old wooden buildings. "We really do need to find a different dealer."

"Who though?"

"Fair point." Ricketts had been the only one willing to sell to us on an installment plan.

Which meant we were stuck relying on a guy who was as

likely to kill us as help us.

Ana drove the buggy onto the flat ground of the desert and sped toward the town. I stayed alert as we neared. It might be our home, but it hadn't felt that way since Ricketts had sent his bone crackers to scare us.

"We really need to move," I muttered.

"And go where? Our magic is too unstable to be safe outside of the valley."

"My magic, you mean." I was the one who blew shit up.

"Not like I'm going to ditch you." Ana scoffed. "Anyway, without you, I'm nothing but a shield. We need your firepower to make a living. So yeah, here we stay."

I grinned, my chest filling with warmth. Ana was right—there were practical reasons that we stayed in Death Valley. But the fact of the matter was—there would always be a *we*. Ana and I were a team.

Ana drove the buggy down the main street of town. It was straight out of an old western movie, with a packed dirt road, wooden buildings, and even a saloon called The Death's Door.

A tumbleweed bounced across the road as a couple of the old timers sitting on the saloon's porch tipped their hats to us. It'd taken us years to earn that honor. Which was fair. The old coots had once been some of the toughest dudes around. Before our time, at least.

Death Valley Junction was full of outlaws. But if you really needed to hide out, then you caught a ride with us across Death Valley. We'd take anyone who could pay, delivering them to Hider's Haven, where the real outlaws lived.

We were the only ones brave enough to risk the trip. Therefore, we earned the honor of a hat tip.

Ana turned onto our street. She parked the buggy in the patch of dirt at the side of our rundown house. It was a one-story affair, built of weathered brown wood with a broken step leading up to the magically reinforced door.

I leapt out of the buggy and hustled inside, Ana following right behind. I ran a wary gaze over the interior of the house. We were in the kitchen, but I could see the living room at the back of the house.

Same crappy old furniture... Check.

Same unpaid bills on the counter... Check.

Picture of Mom and Rowan on the empty TV table... Check.

Whelp, that was it. We didn't own anything else of value besides our enchanted weapons, and we carried those with us at all times, stored inside the ether and ready to be drawn out of thin air when we needed them. That spell had cost a pretty penny, but it'd been worth it.

Ana rubbed the back of her neck and headed toward the fridge. I followed.

"Really feels like something is about to blow any minute, doesn't it?" She grabbed a cold bottle of beer out of the fridge and tossed it to me, then took one for herself. "These are the last ones, so enjoy them."

"Will do." It wasn't froufrou cocktails like I preferred, but those had gone out of the budget years ago.

I popped open the beer, took a swig, then poked in the cabinets for some food. I frowned, shoulders drooping.

Pretty barren, just like the fridge. Not even PB&J. Or candy sandwiches, as I liked to call them.

With my stomach grumbling, I sat in the rickety chair and propped my boots on the table, then sighed. "I wish there was something we could do about Ricketts and his bone crackers."

Just thinking about it made fear buzz under my skin. Made my stomach turn. When I was afraid, I liked to take action. Jump into it.

But at the moment, there was nothing to do but wait. Couldn't even sleep in security.

It was torture.

"We need those concealment charms, so we have to keep him

happy." Ana leaned over the kitchen sink and looked out the window, clearly checking for our stalkers. "You remember what Mom said before she died."

"Yeah. We can't be exposed. And Ricketts wouldn't hesitate to cut the magic to our charms."

At least Ricketts was someone we knew.

The unknown was scarier. We had no idea what had happened to Rowan five years ago. Though we'd searched—spending most of the money meant for our concealment charm payments—we'd never found her.

Honestly, we thought she was dead, captured by those we hid from.

My throat tightened.

Rowan.

I drew in a shuddery breath, forcing away the pain. She might not be dead.

Maybe.

"Uh, Bree?" Ana's voice broke through the sad soup of my memories.

My gaze jerked up to her. "Yeah?"

She turned from the window, her gaze stark. "The bone crackers are here."

Cold fear flowed through my veins. My muscles tensed and my mind went on alert as I carefully swung my legs off the table and stood. It felt like I moved in slow motion.

I was almost relieved—finally, the waiting was over. "How many?"

"Six. And I'm feeling more magical signatures, so I think there's more."

"Shit." My heart thundered as I walked to the window.

At worst, Ricketts sent two to scare us. But six?

That was unheard of.

Six wasn't a warning. Six was...death.

I leaned over the sink and looked out the window. The

packed-dirt street was empty except for six mages. Each lazily tossed a fireball in the air.

Fire Mages.

In a wooden town.

Staring at our wooden house.

"He's come to make an example of us," I said. We hadn't paid up in months, instead using our money on a lead for Rowan that hadn't panned out.

"We don't have the payment."

"And we've hocked everything of value already."

"Except the buggy."

My stomach soured. "We give him that and we're dead. No way to make a living means we'll be in this situation next month when it's time to pay up."

"So you're saying we run for it?"

A blast sounded. Debris exploded out from the corner of the kitchen.

I leapt back.

One of the mages tossing blue balls of energy into the air had clearly gotten sick of waiting and had hurled one toward the house.

I stared at the hole in the wall. Outside, sunlight shined on the dirt. I swallowed hard. "Yep! Time to run. The time for negotiating is past. We can do a couple more jobs in the desert and use that money to buy ourselves some time."

"Sounds risky. But since the alternative is that they blow up the house with us inside..." Ana grimaced. "I'm in."

"Good." If I was going to go down, it'd be in a blaze of glory, rescuing some baby bald eagles or something heroic. Not as a barbecued example made by a Blood Sorcerer.

I leaned to get a better look out the window. The Fire Mages were tossing their fireballs more quickly, deadly jugglers impatient to start their act. My heart thundered, and my skin grew cold.

Another energy ball plowed straight toward the kitchen window, as if someone had seen me peering out.

A scream caught in my throat as I threw myself to the floor, trying to avoid the blast of wooden shards splintering out from the wall.

"Time to go!" I scrambled to my feet, Ana following.

We crawled to the back door, staying low to avoid the windows and darting around debris. In the living room, I grabbed the picture frame off the otherwise empty TV table and yanked the picture out, shoving it in my jacket pocket. It was the only image we had of our mother and Rowan. If these guys bombed our place, no way I wanted to lose it.

I hurried to join Ana, then crouched at the door and looked at her. I swallowed my fear. "You shield and I'll blast?"

She nodded. "On three."

We counted down, then burst out of the door. Because our lives were generally screwed up, we'd practiced this, knowing that one day, our luck would run out and someone would find us here.

Like clockwork, we did as we'd trained, Ana going high and me going low, like the SWAT team on TV. It was where we'd learned our moves, back when we'd had a TV.

She threw out her hands and her magic exploded outward, creating a glimmering force field that shielded us from oncoming blows.

Ten feet from us, there was a man. He was tall and slender, wearing an overcoat that must be torture in this heat. He raised his hand, and a blue glass potion bomb glinted in the light.

Dark magic radiated from the thing, stinking like a fish in a sewer.

Only deadly potion bombs smelled *that* bad.

"You're gonna die, girlie," he growled, voice thick with malevolence.

"Girlie?" I snarled at him.

I drew my sword and shield from the ether, not wanting to waste magic on someone so close. His eyes widened at the sight of the steel. He moved to hurl his potion bomb, but I was too fast, raising my shield and darting toward him. I stabbed him through the heart.

He gurgled and grunted, blood pouring down his chest. The deadly potion bomb dropped to the ground, and I dodged the splash. I yanked my blade free and kicked him backward. He tumbled into the dirt, sprawling on his back.

"Shouldn't stand so close to the enemy," I said. "Because I'm fast."

I raced back behind Ana's shield and stashed my sword in the ether.

"Nice one," she said.

"Thanks." I was good with my sword, though I hated to kill. But that guy had made his plans clear. Frankly, I'd rather it be him than me and Ana.

"There!" Ana pointed toward the edge of the house.

A mage had appeared, clearly scouting out the back of the house. He was a skinny man in his forties. His black eyes darted to us, and he grinned, raising his hands. Fire glowed around them, ready to be hurled at us.

At my wooden house.

They were going to *destroy my house.*

We owned almost nothing, and they would take it from us.

My skin chilled as I crouched low and lunged toward the edge of the shield. Behind him, there was nothing but sagebrush, since we lived at the edge of town. I could attack without worrying about blasting away my neighbor's house. I flung a sonic boom toward the man.

He hurled a fireball at the same time. It collided with my magic, the fire exploding in a shower of sparks, before the boom overpowered it and crashed into the mage, throwing him to his back.

13

He stayed down, clearly knocked out.

Good. After our fight across Death Valley, I wasn't fully charged. Every shot had to count.

"To the corner." I hurried toward the edge of the house.

Ana dropped her shield and followed. Like all supernaturals— or the vast majority, at least—her power wasn't infinite either.

We peered around the edge. Relief coursed through me when I saw that the buggy, which was parked at the side of the house, was fine. There was no one near it, and the only damage was from the salt monster earlier today. The enemy congregated at the front of the house, on the main street. From here, I could see at least three, though there'd been more when I'd looked from the kitchen window.

One of the mages, who was tossing his fireball in the air, caught sight of us, his blue gaze going bright with interest. We had to get away from the house so his fire wouldn't light up our home. I couldn't bear to lose it.

"Shield!" I said.

Steaming noon sun burned down on us as Ana threw up her shield, a shimmering barrier about seven feet tall and four feet wide. Sticking side by side, we darted out from behind the house, staying between it and the buggy, not wanting to draw their fire toward either of our only possessions.

The mage hurled his flame at us, clearly not able to see the shield or not caring. It exploded against the luminescent surface that protected us, a shower of sparks raining onto the dirt.

The surprise and anger in his eyes confirmed what I'd suspected—he hadn't seen the shield. Only a few supernaturals seemed to be able to.

I shifted to the edge of the shield, just enough that I could send a sonic boom toward him. It exploded out of me, blasting through the air to collide with his legs. The shock reverberated up his body, making him shake like a rag doll in a tornado.

He crashed to the ground, unable to even shout.

I winced, a little bit horrified by my own power. Sure, he was here to kill us and I wasn't about to let that happen. But I was used to using my magic against monsters and inanimate objects. Seeing it hurt a person like that was…disturbing.

A blast of blue energy plowed into Ana's shield, driving the worry from my mind.

"Only twenty feet to go," I murmured, edging toward the buggy.

Ana strained to keep her shield up. When a mage approached with his flame, I raised my hands to blast him, but something plowed into me from behind. Electricity shot up my spine, pain tearing through me. I crashed to the ground on my front, skidding on the dirt. Beside me, Ana sprawled out.

Bells clanged in my ears. I blinked, trying to clear my vision. Panic surged as I played dead, surveying our surroundings. Ana was out cold, prone on the dirt next to me. She'd taken the brunt of the hit. Electric shock, I was pretty sure. Painful, but at least it hadn't been fire.

The bastards were slowly approaching, their gazes riveted to us. Their hands no longer glowed with magic—they probably wanted to poke us with sticks to see if we were really dead. Which bought me a few precious seconds.

It felt like time slowed. Adrenaline raced through me. This was it—I had only seconds and we were surrounded.

I scrambled to my feet. Pain twisted my muscles as I grabbed Ana's arm and dragged her limp form across the dirt, heaving with everything I had. Before the mages could power up their magic, we were behind the buggy, Ana still out cold.

Unfortunately, the protected side of the buggy was also the side that had been damaged by the salt monster. The damaged poison-coated spikes bent over the door, locking it closed. I could carefully climb up and over, slipping into the cockpit and driving off, but there was no way I could drag Ana over the spikes without the Ravener poison getting her.

I shook Ana. "Get up!"

She lay still as a rock.

"Get up!"

Still nothing.

Dang it. I had no more time. I could run for it solo, but I'd rather throw myself onto the Ravener poisoned spikes than leave Ana behind.

"Come oooouuut!" one of the mages sang.

His tone made me want to pull his tongue out.

Panting, I peered around the edge of the buggy. Four mages approached— two with glowing blue hands, and two with fire. Though the electric shock blasts would hurt like hell, it was the fire mages who really had me worried. One well-placed fireball could blow the buggy—and us—to smithereens if it hit the engine.

"One shot," I muttered. That was all I had to take them all out, and they stood between me and my house, four of them about to fire.

I swallowed hard, calling on my magic and letting it grow inside me. With a desperate prayer to whatever fates were listening, I darted out to hurl it at the mages.

But a fifth mage—he must have crept up behind the other because I hadn't seen him—threw a blue potion bomb toward us. I heaved my sonic boom at the mage, aiming for his blue leather jacket and hoping to stop his potion bomb. The force of the magic exploding out of me made me stumble backward.

The sonic boom that I'd thrown crashed into my attackers, colliding with them like a freight train.

They flew backward, their bodies slamming into the wooden wall of my house. Along with the rest of my sonic boom. It crashed into the wall, sending wood and glass flying. The house exploded into thousands of pieces of wood and glass. It rained down like a terrible hail.

Too much magic.

The four attackers were dead now. But so was my house.

Hot tears pricked my eyes. I'd expected that maybe they would trash our house. Not that *I'd* do it.

That place had been a hell hole, but it'd been *our* hell hole.

I stepped backward, horrified. Something crunched underfoot. I looked down—shards of the blue potion bomb.

Oh, shit.

And my side was wet and cold. I touched it, then raised my damp hand to my nose. A blue potion gleamed on my fingertips and smelled like sweet, rotten fish.

An impossible, terrible smell that sent terror streaking through me.

I'd heard of this—the poison that Ricketts used when he was done with you. It'd kill you in weeks unless you went to him to get the antidote. Most people didn't even bother to go get it, because whatever he'd do to you when he got you…

Fear chilled my skin.

We should have paid him the money we owed.

I turned to Ana, who was still sprawled in the dirt.

Shards of blue glass were scattered around her, and her shirt was wet, too.

"No!" I fell to my knees at her side.

She'd been hit!

The potion bomb must have avoided my sonic boom and exploded on the ground between us, splattering us both. I'd been so obsessed with our destroyed house that I hadn't noticed.

I shook Ana's shoulder, throat closed tight with fear. "Wake up!"

She was limp as a dishrag. Frantic, I felt for a pulse at her neck. It was steady and strong, thank fates.

I peered around the buggy. My house was a pile of rubble, so I could see the front street that had previously been obscured. There were six other mages, all of whom turned to look toward us.

17

My heart thundered in my ears as I called on my magic, only to find the well empty.

I'd used it all up.

Shit. Sweat broke out on my skin. *Shit, shit, shit.*

We were rats in a trap, and I was just as scared. All the danger and monsters I'd faced out in Death Valley were nothing compared to this.

Oh, man, we needed to run for it. We had to find an antidote to this poison that didn't involve Ricketts. Above all, we couldn't be captured and brought to him. We'd be defenseless.

But we couldn't run. There was no way I could haul Ana into the buggy without the Ravener poison getting her.

But what if I went from the front? That was slightly shielded.

I pulled a bandana out of my pocket and grabbed up some of the glass shards from the potion bomb. We needed to identify the exact poison if we made it out of here. Then I reached down to grab her arm, and pulled. I managed to get her to the front of the buggy, but it was impossible to haul her over the hood.

My strength, along with my magic, had waned so much that we were now sitting ducks. Terror tightened my throat.

A flash of movement caught my eye.

I glanced toward the street. Four more people had arrived. Three were pretty normal, but one was…

Holy shit.

The fourth one—a man well over six feet tall—had a magical signature that smacked me in the face like a wrecking ball. He was danger and violence and *power*. And hot as hell, with dark hair and blazing green eyes set over sharp cheekbones.

I shivered, my mouth suddenly dry.

If I thought Ricketts's goons were scary, they were nothing compared to this man.

Then he turned and looked straight at me.

CHAPTER TWO

Well, now I knew we were gonna die.

If this was Ricketts's finishing team…

We were done for.

A terrible thought flashed in my mind.

Oh, hell.

Were these the people we'd been hiding from all these years? The reason my mother had run with us after they'd attacked our childhood home?

It was more than possible. Since Ricketts had decided to make an example of us, he likely would have cut the magic that fed our concealment charms. Which would make it possible for the bogeyman to find us.

And *this* guy could definitely be the bogeyman we'd feared.

He turned from me, his gaze sweeping over my assailants, who looked at him like he was the devil come to Earth to collect on their sins. The man—Sexy McScary—pointed to the three farthest from me.

His companions jumped into action, moving so quickly that they were obviously pros. For the first time, I actually noticed them as more than just faceless sidekicks. Two men, both about my age and tall and lanky, darted toward two of Ricketts's men. Then they disappeared into the air.

One moment they were there, and the next, they were gone.

The two fire mages that they'd been running toward suddenly turned their magic on themselves, lighting a massive fire and leaping into it.

Oh, hell no!

Whatever those two new guys could do... I wanted no part of it.

I turned my gaze toward the woman who was with them.

She was tall and slim, with short platinum hair and icy gray eyes. She sprinted for the last of the three men, raising her palms and shooting a narrow jet of water at the man. It plowed into his chest, then came out the other side, tinged pink with blood. He toppled onto his back.

My stomach turned.

Holy fates, she could shoot water so fast that it pierced a person straight through. What the heck *was* she? I'd never even heard of a power like that.

But if I'd thought she was scary, it was nothing compared to Sexy McScary. Whose nickname suddenly seemed way too inane for him. He was violence personified.

He stalked toward the last three mages, black smoke rolling out from his feet with every step. The earth seemed to shake with the hoofbeats of a thousand war stallions. Visions of battle and blood flashed in my mind's eye. The three mages just stood and stared at him, as entranced as I was. Probably also frozen with fear.

Finally, they seemed to shake themselves out of it, faces pale and hands trembling. They raised their palms, which glowed with fire and blue electric magic. As a group, they hurled their weapons at the man who stalked toward them.

The terrifying warrior was twenty feet from them, and entirely unarmed. As if in slow motion, the fireballs and electric energy flew toward him. He raised one muscular arm, and an ancient-looking round shield appeared. The fire and electricity plowed into it.

He didn't even falter, just kept charging toward them, picking up speed. Faster and faster.

The mages had powered up more fireballs and electricity by the time he neared them, but they never had a chance to deploy their weapons. The man hurled the shield off his arm like a boomerang.

It flew through the air, turning as it reached the mages and slicing off their heads. My jaw dropped as their heads flew into the air, blood spurting. The shield turned again, flying back to the man, who caught it.

The bodies of the mages collapsed in the dirt. I sank hard onto my butt.

Fear like I'd never known raced through me, chilling my bones until I thought they might crack. Had he helped us or cleared the way to get to us? If it was the latter…

I can't fight them.

I stood literally no chance against a warrior like that. I couldn't fight *any* of them, not with my magic depleted. *I can't do it.*

Beside me, Ana groaned, then lay still once again.

Shit.

Can't wasn't going to get us anywhere. Ana needed me. And the fear in my chest drove me to action, as it always did.

Fight first, questions later.

I swallowed hard and climbed shakily to my feet.

The warrior turned toward me, along with his three compatriots. His blue eyes landed on me, and he approached. The black smoke no longer rolled out from beneath his feet and the thunder of warhorse hooves had disappeared, but he was still in fight mode.

A guy like him was *always* in fight mode.

I edged away from the buggy—no need to risk my last possession, or Ana—and called upon every scrap of magic I had left. It vibrated inside me, desperate to be set free—as if it, too, knew that this was our only shot.

I hurled the power at him, the sonic boom exploding out of me. It wasn't much—just the dregs of my magic—but any size sonic boom was usually pretty good.

It smashed into all four of them, bowling the two men and the woman off their feet. They landed hard in the dirt, skidding backward.

But the man didn't budge. He just kept walking.

Shit.

That had never happened before.

I glanced down at Ana. *I'm so sorry.*

Then I turned to the man, straightening my shoulders. There wasn't an ounce of magic left in me, but I still had my sword stashed in the ether. I just needed to find a time to use it.

As he stalked toward me, his magical signatures filled the air. Each supernatural had a magical signature that was uniquely theirs. They hit the senses—taste, smell, touch. That sort of thing. Very strong supernaturals had more than one signature.

This guy had all five.

The scent of a storm at sea filled my nose, and the taste of tart apples touched my tongue. His magic sounded like the clang of swords in battle and felt like a caress against my skin.

I shivered.

It took all I had to ignore it and focus on the aura that radiated from him. Black and silver—it was a strange one. I'd never seen any like it.

In fairness, I'd seen only a few auras in my life. They were the rarest signature of all.

He stopped about ten feet from me, sizing me up.

Fair enough, since I was doing the same to him.

He was built like violence personified but was insanely handsome in a way that warmed me and made me feel like a giant idiot at the same time. He was dangerous, and he looked it.

His black hair gleamed in the sunlight, and his green eyes glinted with interest. But it was his full lips that softened his harsh face, drawing my gaze.

I was attracted and scared and pissed, all at the same. It was a sickening combo, to be honest.

At some point, his friends had rejoined him, but they lingered about ten feet back, as if making it clear that he was the boss and they were backup.

His gaze dropped to Ana, who lay in the dirt a few feet from me. I stepped toward her, getting in the way.

"You protect your friend?" he asked, his rough voice tinged with a sexy Scottish accent.

"Obviously, you moron." *Well, that wasn't a great start.*

The corner of his full lips quirked up. "I expected a thank-you, not insults."

"A thank-you?"

"For killing your attackers."

"Ha. I had that under control." So maybe he *was* helping us?

"Hmmm." His eyes sparkled as he glanced toward my destroyed house. "Aye."

I scowled, but was happy to let him believe that Ricketts's men had done that. Not me, no way. "Who the hell are you?"

"I'm Cade, and I am here to collect you."

"Collect?" My heart thundered. They were here to *collect* us? These folks didn't seem like the people we'd run from as children —they were too young, and their magic didn't smell evil, like our pursuers' did. Still... "I'm not super interested in being collected."

I looked around, hoping against hope that the town's residents would rise up to protect us. But no way in hell that was going to happen. Death Valley Junction was a last resort kind of town. One where you came if you were in trouble. Hence, it was full of outlaws minding their own business. We might get a hat tip, but no backup. The closest thing we had to family or friends here was an old man we'd befriended when we'd first arrived. But he was too old to launch an attack, and I wouldn't want him to risk himself like that. So that was out.

"Come." Cade stepped forward, his hand outstretched.

Seriously? I was dealing with a destroyed house and deadly poisoning and now these folks?

"Hmmm." I tapped my chin as I stepped back, mind racing. Stalling for an idea. Or lulling him away from the hyper vigilance he wore like a cloak. Waiting for Ana to wake. I wasn't sure what I was stalling for yet—just that I needed some kind of advantage. "Not interested. Especially when you haven't explained who you are."

"I represent the Undercover Protectorate. We'd like to make you an offer."

The name rang a bell, but I couldn't place it. I quirked a brow. "One I can't refuse?"

The woman behind him huffed a laugh.

"Aye." He nodded.

Beside me, Ana shifted slightly. Waking? She'd do it quietly, hoping to have the advantage. I knew her like I knew myself, and that was what I'd do. But what about the poison?

On the ground, her hand formed a peace sign.

Our symbol.

Fight time.

It was ironic that we'd chosen the peace sign for when we would launch an attack, but we'd always been a little weird. Like our SWAT team formation from earlier, this was a holdover from when we knew we'd have to run for it eventually.

I shifted left, making sure to draw his eyes away from her. "Well, I refuse."

"You haven't heard it."

I darted my gaze to the left of his shoulder, forcing my eyes wide and my expression horrified. As expected, he turned to look.

I drew my sword from the ether, the magical atmosphere that surrounded us, and sliced it toward him. I'd wound him enough to distract his colleagues, then we'd run for it in the buggy.

Ana jumped up as I'd known she would, then crouched, ready to fight or flee.

But as my blade neared him, Cade reached out without even turning, catching the shining steel in his hand.

Holy fates!

I jerked at my blade, but he gripped it tightly. No blood seeped from his palm—though it *should*. My sword could cut through metal.

"What the hell?"

He turned to me, his gaze heavy. "Don't try it. You can't beat me."

"Are you a robot?"

His lips quirked up in a sexy smile. "Hardly."

From behind him, the two men laughed. They had dark hair and golden skin, both of them pretty enough to be in a boy band.

The one on the left smiled. "Strength of a robot, maybe."

Butt smoocher.

Ana moved closer to me so her shield could block us both. Sweat dotted her forehead. "I don't know what you're offering, but I heard Bree refuse, so I'm out, too."

The scary water woman's mouth quirked up in a smile.

"That's not an option. You're coming with us. It's not safe to speak here, but we'll explain when we arrive back at headquarters," Cade said.

"You want us to come to some mysterious place with you, a guy who isn't hurt by swords? That's literally the worst offer I've ever gotten, and I was once offered a night in the sack with a guy named Big Monkey. He had no teeth, and his knuckles dragged on the ground. So let's just say I know a bad offer when I see one." Out of the corner of my mouth, I whispered to Ana, "Shield us to the buggy. Now."

She threw out her hands, her shield bursting forth. We raced for the buggy, which was only six feet away. We could make it. We had to make it.

Cade was fast, though. He was on us in seconds, somehow breaking through Ana's shield. Her magic faded entirely.

What the hell!

Something was really wrong with her. That poison...

I swung my blade, slicing his shoulder. The deep cut welled with blood, but he moved faster, so quickly I almost couldn't see him. His strong arms wrapped around me, pinning my sword arm to my side.

One of the other men was on Ana a moment later.

I thrashed and struggled, but his iron grip kept me immobile. His heat burned through me, making my heart pound and rage rise in my chest. "Let me go!"

Ana shrieked, managing to get an elbow into the face of the man who held her.

"Rat bastards!" she shouted.

"Ah, ah. I'll have you know that my parentage is sound!" The man grinned.

"He's 100 percent moron! Both sides!" The platinum-haired woman crowed.

These people were *nuts*. I thrashed in Cade's iron grip, desperation fueling me. But he didn't budge, the cage of his arms somehow gentle despite their permanence.

The woman stepped forward, digging into her pocket. She pulled out a small black stone.

A transport stone.

"No!" I screamed.

She chucked it to the ground, and glittering smoke rose up. Cade dragged me into it, and the ether sucked me in, sending me on a whirlwind ride through space. My head spun as the blackness surrounded me.

A moment later, I stumbled on solid ground. Cade released me, and I went to my knees in soggy, cold grass.

I shivered and scrambled to my feet, spinning around.

My heart calmed—just slightly—when I saw Ana next to me. She'd managed to maintain her footing, but probably only because her captor still held her.

All around us, mountains soared, stretching into the distance. Steep and dusty green, they were freaking amazing. Sweeps of purple covered their sides, and in a deep valley a sparkling river wound toward the horizon. The air was cool and wet, gray clouds hanging low.

We were *so* not in Death Valley anymore.

"Where are we?" I demanded. There wasn't a single building, road, or car in sight.

"Scotland. The far north," Cade said.

"Otherwise known as the ass end of nowhere." The woman grinned, then sauntered over and stuck out her hand. "I'm Caro."

I stared at her hand like it was a snake, then met her silver eyes. "You have to be joking. You just abducted me. I'm not about to make nice."

She shrugged, clearly not bothered. "You'll come around."

"They all do! We did," one of the men said. He let go of Ana, and she darted away, stumbling toward me.

There was only one reason they'd let go of us. There was nowhere to go. Not for miles, probably.

The dark-haired man smiled. "I'm Ali."

"And I'm Haris," the other said.

"What are you?" I demanded, remembering their creepy power.

"Djinn," they both said.

At my blank look, Ali said, "People think we're genies, but we don't do wishes. Just invisibility and possessing people."

They'd made those mages kill themselves.

I backed up. "Stay the hell away from me, then."

"Seconded," Ana said.

"Don't worry about us," Haris said.

I'd be the judge of that. "We're in the Highlands, then?"

Ali glanced at the mountains around. "What gave it away?"

"Funny." I shot him the hairy eyeball.

"You can't walk out of here," Cade said. "So you may as well come with us and hear what we have to say."

"I'm not afraid to walk." I stepped back from him, wanting to put as much distance as I could between myself and the sexy supernatural of indeterminate—but terrifying—species. I made it three steps before I hit an invisible barrier. "What the hell?"

"You're on our land," Cade said. "Until you're within the castle, you can't go far from us."

Caro winked.

A freaking wink? She was nuts.

"Come on." Cade turned and set off across the side of the mountain. "We'll explain it all when we're within the walls. It's safer there."

The others followed. When they were about ten feet away from us, immense pressure formed at my back, forcing me to follow. Ana kept in step with me, dragged along in the same way.

If only my magic weren't depleted, maybe I could blast out of this. We'd just have to go along until we had the strength to fight our way out.

"What the heck is happening?" Ana whispered. "Who are these people?"

"I have no idea." I studied Cade's impossibly broad shoulders. "I don't think they're Ricketts's men, since they killed the bastards. But are they the people that Mom warned us about?"

"They don't seem like the ones who came for us when we were children," Ana said. "Their magic doesn't feel the same. Not evil. But dangerous."

I still remembered running with our mother, the dark magic pursuing us. We'd made it away, barely, but never been able to return home.

"Let's reserve judgment." I met her worried gaze. "Because we have bigger problems."

"Than abduction?"

"Yeah. While you were unconscious, we were both poisoned by that stuff Ricketts uses to force you to go to him."

Her face paled. "The poison that turns you to stone?"

"I think so. It smelled like it." We'd heard it described before by other horrified outlaws who'd gone to Ricketts for help. Like we stupidly had.

"Why does he want us to go to him?" she asked. "To make us pay up? We can't do that without a job or money."

"No idea. Something weird is happening. We just need to..." My words trailed off as we turned a bend on the mountainside.

"Holy fates," Ana breathed.

A castle spread out before us, a monstrosity built of gray stone and black slate. The exterior wall soared high, but the towers were even higher, piercing the gray sky. The place was impossibly huge, and magic sparked around it, almost like it was a living thing.

I picked my jaw up off the floor in time to notice Caro staring at us. "Pretty cool, huh?"

"It's all right." It was more than *all right*. It was incredible.

And I really didn't want to go inside those walls. Because even though it looked like a fantasy on steroids, there'd be no getting out of there.

But our captors kept walking, and we kept being dragged along behind. I dug my heels into the dirt, sweat breaking out on my skin. But it did no good—the spell dragged me along behind them.

"I hate this freaking spell," Ana muttered, a single bead of sweat rolling down her face.

"Seconded." I panted, then finally gave up fighting and walked. I needed to conserve my strength, and my chest was starting to ache.

Was that the poison? I shuddered.

Caro sauntered back to join.

"Not bad, eh?" Caro said.

"I'm not a fan."

"You will be." She grinned. "I was skeptical first, too, but now I'm a convert."

"Like a cult?" This was getting weird.

"Nah, you'll see." She winked.

The two Djinn were goofing off in the distance, laughing their heads off and clearly comfortable now that they were home. Cade walked with purpose.

Caro studied Ana. "Are you doing all right?"

"Fine." But Ana's voice wavered. Her color was paler than usual.

Was she feeling the effects of the poison too?

"Are you sure?" Caro pointed to the guys. "One of the guys could carry you."

"I'm *fine.*"

Neither of us were, but I understood her need to put on a show of strength. I wrapped an arm around her waist, and we helped each other walk. My pain wasn't too bad, but it did ache. I hoped hers wasn't worse.

I looked at Caro, appreciating the concern she was showing to Ana. These people weren't acting like evil abductors. "You're really not going to kill us?"

She shook her head. "No."

Hmmm. I almost believed her.

But maybe that was my desperation talking, because we were at a serious low point. My magic hadn't renewed enough to make an escape yet. This situation might be bad, but what we were running from was far worse. So it looked like we'd be getting a tour of the castle.

They led us up to a massive gate and stopped in front of it. Cade laid a big hand against the sturdy wood and murmured a few words I couldn't hear.

The gate groaned and creaked as it rose.

Ana and I followed Cade through the gate, everyone else behind us. The wall was so wide that it felt like passing through a tunnel. Magic sparked over my skin, some kind of protective spell that would keep out unwelcome visitors. If I could feel it and I'd been invited, that meant it was strong as hell.

There was no way Ricketts could get through here without an inside man. If he could even find it out here in the boonies, which I sincerely doubted.

I leaned toward Ana and whispered, "If this wasn't a crazy cult, it'd be a great hideout."

She nodded. "You read my mind."

A massive stretch of land sprawled out ahead of us. It was huge, indicating that the castle compound was far bigger than I'd realized. Due to magic expanding the space within, if I had to guess.

In the middle of the open space, about a hundred meters away on a hill, sat the biggest castle I'd ever seen. It was a monstrosity of towers and massive halls, so huge that it'd probably take decades to learn it all. Magic sparked from the place, rolling over the land.

I could see no wall behind the castle. Was it on a cliff?

I sniffed the air, getting a hint of the sea.

It was.

Wow.

We had to be at the very top of Scotland.

To the left, there was a small forest contained entirely within the castle's exterior wall. On the right were some old buildings. Stables, maybe.

"Follow me," Cade said.

I blinked, realizing that he'd been staring at us. Concern creased his brow.

Then Ana keeled over, headed for the ground.

Cade was on us in seconds, sweeping her up.

Fear lanced through me, sharp and cold. "Ana!"

"What's wrong with her?" he demanded, concern in his voice.

Ana's eyes opened, and she thrashed in his arms, punching his chest. "Let me down! I was just lightheaded for a moment."

He set her down gently. To be honest, I didn't hate the careful way he held my sister.

Cade's nose wrinkled. "No, there's something else here." His eyes widened. "Poison?"

"Are you all right?" Caro demanded.

The two Djinn approached, concern drawing their eyebrows together.

Cade's voice snapped into action mode. "We're going to Hedy, our resident witch and inventor. She'll help."

"Why do you care, if you abducted us?" I demanded.

"Normally we don't abduct. We discuss," Cade said. "But those were extenuating circumstances. I know a runner when I see one. And if you got on that vehicle of yours, you'd be in your element. Nearly impossible to catch."

Fair enough. After facing down Ricketts's men, we'd been primed to run or fight to the death, no question.

We'd never have expected *help*.

Which was what these people were promising.

I was skeptical.

But we needed to consider it, since we were fresh out of options. We were chock-full of poison with no home, no money, no car, and currently no magic.

Thinking on my feet and trusting my instincts had saved us countless times in Death Valley. Right now, there was only one reasonable thing to do.

Oh, hell. We had to trust these people. "We'll see your healer."

And if she couldn't help, my magic should be recouped enough soon that we'd blast our way out of this place somehow and start fresh.

He nodded, pleased, yet still somehow managing to look dangerous and grim. I shivered, not wanting to be attracted to him but failing miserably.

He turned and strode toward a squat tower that was set near the entrance gate. Ana and I hurried to follow, Caro at my side. The two Djinn followed behind. Their concern made me uncomfortable.

Sure, we smelled of sweet, rotten fish, so something was *clearly* up. But they didn't know us.

Why would they care about us?

Cade led us to a large tower sitting relatively close to the gate. I followed him inside. Caro, Ali, and Haris waited outside.

The room within was large and round, empty except for several chairs. The lack of windows would have made it dark, but there were glowing glass spheres floating near the ceiling, shedding a golden light on the space. Near the wall, a metal spiral staircase led up to another floor.

"Why does this remind me of a dungeon?" I asked.

"It's not." The voice sounded from above. Feminine, but deep. Footsteps thudded, then a person appeared on the spiral staircase. She was in her late twenties, with silver hair tipped in lavender and wearing a flowing black dress. "This is where I work on new magic. Magic that cannot be allowed to escape through any pesky windows."

I let my senses detect the magical signatures that filled the place. Almost everything was pleasant, indicating that she didn't dabble in dark magic.

"Who are you?" I asked.

She reached the ground floor and approached, her black dress fluttering. "Hedy. The more important question is—are you who I think you are?"

I shared a glance with Ana before replying. "No idea."

She stopped in front of me, clearly absorbing my magical signature. "You are." She turned to smile at Cade. "Good job. Though you brought them in less than stellar condition."

He inclined his head. "They were like that when I found them."

"It's poison," I said. "Can you tell us how bad it is and if you have an antidote?"

She frowned, her nose wrinkling as she sniffed. "*Oh no.*"

I swallowed hard. "Your bedside manner could do with some work."

"I'll buy you a beer later to make up for it."

Who *were* these people that were so nice and welcoming after they abducted us?

She pulled some scissors out of her pocket. "I'm going to take a sample of your shirt that has the poison on it."

I pointed to my side, and she snipped off a square, then took it to the table against the wall and laid it on a piece of slate. She dashed a few drops of different potions onto the fabric, which sizzled and smoked.

"Shit." She turned to us, a frown creasing her brow. "Lithica poison. You have two weeks before you turn to stone if you don't get the antidote."

As I'd feared. But two weeks was even less time than I'd expected. "Do you have it?"

"No. Only one person has it." She gestured to the fabric. "It's his invention."

Cade's eyes snapped to Hedy. "Ricketts?"

"You know him?" I demanded.

"We've been hunting him for years. Were the people who were attacking you his men? They seemed familiar."

"Yes." I gave him a considering glance. If he didn't like Ricketts...

The enemy of my enemy is my friend, and all that business. *Maybe.*

"What do you know about him?" I demanded.

"Let's discuss that in a moment." His gaze turned to Hedy. "Will you finish?"

"Finish what?" Ana asked.

Hedy pulled a silver stone from her dress pocket and held it up toward us.

I raised my hands and stepped back, skin prickling with wariness.

"Don't worry," Hedy said. "This is just going to check you for any latent magic or spells that might be a threat to the compound. A little invention of mine."

"Invention?"

"Yes. I'm a jack of all trades. Like that fellow in the James Bond movies."

"Q?"

"Exactly."

She hovered the silver stone over my chest. It glowed bright and she frowned. "There's something here."

"A concealment charm?" I asked.

"Yes."

Weird. I'd have expected Ricketts to let the charm fade since he was pissed enough to send his goons after us. I shared a worried glance with Ana.

"There's something else as well," Hedy said. "But I can't tell what it is. A spell that's been there a while. I'm going to take a sample to figure it out."

I didn't like the idea of her taking a sample of anything, but I *really* didn't like the idea of an unknown spell clinging to me.

Hedy drew a little empty vial and a wand from her pocket.

I nearly vibrated as I stood still, waiting for her to take the sample. *Please don't involve cutting anything off of me.*

"You use a wand?" I asked. I'd never seen one before. Contrary to popular human myth, witches didn't use wands. Nor did any other variety of supernatural.

"For this, yes. It's another of my inventions." She then poked me in the chest with her wand.

"Hey! Ouch."

"Relax." She muttered a few words in a language I didn't understand.

Something tugged at my chest. The wand's tip glowed as she moved it away from me, then stuck it in the bottle. It glowed within the glass. She corked it and stuck it in her pocket, then did the same to Ana.

Then she went to the desk and picked up two little black bottles and handed them to us. "Lithica poison is painful. It'll be a steady ache that flares occasionally. You'll be turning to stone from the inside out. Take this when the pain becomes too much. Not sooner. It will keep you functioning until you can get the antidote."

Ana and I took the potions, glancing worriedly at each other.

"Thank you." I smiled at her, then turned to Cade and Ana. "Now let's start talking about Ricketts."

I wanted to get a feel for these people ASAP, because if they couldn't help us, we needed to get going on our own.

"We'll go up to the castle and meet with the others," Cade said. "It's the best place to hear our offer."

I looked at Ana, who nodded immediately. And that was the crux of it. We didn't have a lot of options. Any options, really. Even if Cade weren't forcing us to hear his offer, we were poisoned, broke, and the devil was on our tail.

"Fine. We'll go there." I scowled, already wondering if I'd signed up for trouble.

CHAPTER THREE

We followed Cade and Hedy out of the tower and up the slope of the mountain toward the massive castle. As we walked, the clouds parted to reveal a warm yellow sun. It was nothing like Death Valley, where the arrival of the sun meant sweating and eventual death if you weren't on your guard.

No, this was warm and lovely. Even the damp grass beneath my feet was nice. The crisp breeze cooled my cheeks. I'd bet this place would be intense in the winter, but in August, it was pretty sweet.

Despite the lovely weather and beautiful surroundings, power and wealth radiated from this place.

They had all the resources we lacked.

I gave Cade a sidelong glance, taking in his powerful stride and confident gaze. This was a guy for whom the world stopped.

Well, I wasn't going to be one of the stoppers. "So, what exactly are you?"

He glanced at me. "Errand boy."

"Sure." I'd believe that when Ana let me have the last slice of pizza. But since he clearly wasn't going to cooperate, I shifted tactics. "When was this place built? And what the hell is it?"

"It was built nearly a thousand years ago, though there have been renovations." His green eyes met mine. "And you'll learn the rest very shortly."

"You'd better be taking us to the queen or something," I said. "Only royalty would be worth all this trouble."

"*Is* this Balmoral?" Ana frowned skeptically. "Somehow, I'm doubtful. The landscaping is lacking."

"Too hodgepodge." I stifled a laugh. We might be poisoned and slowly turning into stone, but we were clearly going to handle it how we knew best—suppress the worry with jokes.

That whole 'laugh instead of crying' thing? Yeah, that'd gotten us through some hard times. Now, it was second nature.

Cade grinned. "I doubt you'll be unimpressed."

We neared the massive castle that was built of huge blocks of gray stone. Sparkling mullioned glass shone in the windows. A large courtyard paved in great slabs of granite led up to the huge front doors.

Cade led us across the stone courtyard. The massive wooden door swung open as we neared. Magic sparked in the air.

Neat.

Inside, the foyer was huge, with a sweeping, double-sided staircase leading up to a second level. Other doors led off the main entrance room, along with a couple more staircases. A great chandelier shed glittering light over the rough stone walls and floor. Huge paintings hung on the walls, but I didn't take the time to study them.

It was so big and so fantastical that it was hard to get a real handle on it.

A few people climbed the stairs to the second floor, their arms full of heavy books. Others bustled through the main hall, all of them possessing unique magical signatures. Clashing sounds and smells indicated that their magic was all very different.

Everyone turned to stare at us. Some looked mistrusting, others just curious.

"Fancy." I whistled, just to show them I didn't care.

"Practical." Cade turned down the hall to the right. "This way."

I looked at Ana, whose eyes were as round as the full moon.

"This is nuts," she whispered.

"Seconded." We'd never been in a place this nice before. Most of our early life, after running from our original home, had been spent at our homestead cabin in Alaska or Death Valley Junction.

I was having a serious country mouse moment but suppressed it. From here on out, we had to be alert and tough.

As we neared a door at the end of the hallway, varying magical signatures swelled on the air. The smell of old paper, the feeling of a steel sword hilt in my hand, the scent of a wet field. My steps faltered.

"Who's in there?" I demanded.

"We don't go into rooms full of powerful supernaturals that we don't know," Ana said.

"Scared?" Cade asked.

I glared at him. "Smart. We don't like ambushes."

He nodded. "Fair enough. There are four other members of the Undercover Protectorate in the room. Each runs a division of our operations. Their magic is strong because everyone here is strong. But we mean you no harm. We want to make you an offer."

Undercover Protectorate. Why was that name familiar? I focused on the signatures, picking up four. He wasn't lying. I glanced at Ana, who nodded.

"We'll go in, but make it quick," I said. "We obviously don't have a lot of time. And if you make one move against us, I'll blow you apart."

He grinned, sexy as hell and clearly liking my threat.

Weirdo.

I followed him into the room, Ana at my side and Hedy behind us. It was a nicely decorated little library, with a round table in the middle. Four people sat around it. Two men and two women.

One woman caught my eye. Her piercing blue eyes were set off by her dark skin and braids. They sparkled like stars, and were nearly impossible to look away from. There was magic in her eyes, no question. Her scrutiny made the hair on the back of my neck stand up. Man, if she interrogated me, I'd have a hard time not giving up the info she wanted.

The other woman was slender and pale, with magic that smelled of calming lavender. One man was ancient, with stooped shoulders and magic that smelled like the forest, while the other was as bulky as a football player.

Cade lurked toward the back of the room, standing with his arms crossed like a bouncer on duty. His magical power filled the room, making me seriously aware of him.

Hedy stepped forward and gestured to the small crowd. "Bree and Ana, we are the Undercover Protectorate, and these are the heads of the individual divisions of our operation. There's the Demon Trackers Unit, Interspecies Mediation, Research and Development, and the Paranormal Investigative Team."

The Paranormal Investigative Team? The PITs? *Oof.*

Each person nodded at us.

"The five of us are equal here," Hedy said. "But I will speak because you know me best." She pointed to the chairs. "Please, take a seat."

I sat. "I'm going to need you to cut straight to the chase. Because Ana and I don't have a lot of time." We needed to start hunting Ricketts immediately if we wanted a cure in time. I was hoping they could help us, but I wasn't counting on it.

"Bold," Star-eyes said.

"My middle name." I grinned, which was really more of a teeth-baring.

"The Undercover Protectorate was created hundreds of years

ago to protect the magical world from threats, both supernatural and human," Hedy said.

Protect from threats.

Suddenly the pieces slammed together in my head. *That's where I'd heard their name before.* My gaze flashed to Ana, who had paled.

Our mother had spoken of these people. When we'd been running from the ones who'd attacked our home when we were children, aiming to kidnap me and my sisters, our mother had fled with us, saying that she was trying to take us here.

To the secret, fabled organization that protected those in need. That investigated the crimes no one else would. The government certainly wasn't a safe bet for Unknowns like us. But we'd never found the Protectorate, ending up in remote Alaska instead. Our mother had been convinced they'd help us.

I'd always thought that if my mother couldn't find them, then they didn't want to be found.

"Why us?" I asked. Did they know that we were Unknowns? They shouldn't. We'd kept it secret so no one could use that against us. Our mother, a powerful seer, had made it clear that hiding our true selves was vital to our survival.

"We hire only the strongest, rarest supernaturals in the world," Hedy said. "It's one of the reasons we're so secretive. The Order of the Magica doesn't like it when another organization possesses so much power. Whereas they would persecute some of our members, we welcome them."

I nodded, understanding all too well. The government of magic users was committed to keeping magic secret from humans. In their eyes, that meant keeping a handle on the most powerful supernaturals—sometimes by force.

"When we heard of two women willing to fight their way across Death Valley, we became interested," Hedy said. "The strength and skill it took to do that is the kind of thing we want here. We'd like you to join our operation. Train at the academy and then work for one of our divisions."

So they didn't know exactly what we were. Or, they weren't saying.

"We don't want to work for you," Ana said. "We work for ourselves."

"Right now, you won't work for anyone if you don't find a cure for the Lithica poisoning," Hedy said.

Burn.

She turned to the other members of the organization and explained our situation. Frowns spread through the group.

"That is a problem." Star-eyes looked at us. "I'm Jude. I run the Paranormal Investigative Team. Ricketts, the man who poisoned you, has been on our radar for a long time. But we've never been able to catch him. He's too cunning, and his clients are too frightened to speak up. He must really want you if he hit you with the Lithica poison. He only uses that to draw the most powerful to him."

Why did he want us though? To pay our debts? Smelled fishy to me. "So you want to catch him, and you also want us to work for you."

"Yes, though your connection to Ricketts is more of a coincidence," Jude said. "We want you to work for us because you've proven your skill and determination in Death Valley. Ricketts is a bonus."

I nodded, my mind racing. We could use this. We *had* to use this.

Because right now, we were shit out of luck. Poisoned, with no money, no house, no buggy—so no way to get anywhere *or* make a living.

I shared a glance with Ana, able to see the wheels turning in her head. We didn't want to work for these people—we didn't know them. But we could use them.

I hiked my thumb toward Cade. "The big guy back there said

you could help us catch Ricketts. But how? I already know how to find him. What can you do for us?"

I was being a hard ass, but I was also fighting for Ana. Being sweet hadn't gotten me far in life, but being tough? Yeah, that had worked.

"Did the mage who hit you with the poison bomb deliver the address for the antidote?" Jude asked.

"I killed him before he had the chance." I still cringed at the flub. "It happened before I even realized I'd been hit by the potion bomb."

Otherwise, I never would have thrown it. From what I knew, the method was to hit you with the bomb and then tell you where to get the antidote.

So, my bad.

"But I have a contact who can help me find it." I didn't explain more. I couldn't, not without risking my friend. "But I'd like backup in confronting Ricketts when I do find him." My mind raced. "And we'd like your help recovering our truck."

Ana nodded subtly at me, obviously thinking the same thing. If we could use their help to get the cure *and* get the buggy, we'd be in good shape to rebuild our lives once this was over.

"Why would you need your vehicle if you're going to work here?" Cade asked from the side wall.

I went for honesty. "We might not work here." Us working here was as likely as a naked mole rat becoming a sea captain. "But you could prove your goodwill by helping us get our truck back. And say we *did* decide to stick around. We're much stronger with our buggy."

The division leaders looked at each other and nodded, then they looked at Cade. Clearly for his approval.

But if they wanted that, why wasn't he sitting here with them?

I turned around to see him nod, then looked back at the table.

"Normally, when a new recruit joins us, they start out in training," Jude said. "But we've watched you on your trips across the desert. You're the most impressive untrained fighters we've ever seen. You're qualified to hunt Ricketts. And frankly, you need to. I've seen this poison before. It's a nasty one."

"I will accompany you," Cade said. "When we determine that more backup is needed, we'll get it."

My heart thudded. Work with the sexy, kinda scary powerful dude? I both loved that idea and hated it. I also had no choice. I'd played my cards, and now they were playing theirs.

"Fine." I looked at Ana. "You stay and go get the buggy. Make sure it's in good working order. If Ricketts sends more men to our house, they might trash it."

"On it," she said.

The slightest bit of hope lit in my chest. This might actually work out for us. Getting the cure and the buggy would put us in a good position.

And I wasn't worried about splitting from Ana. She was tougher than me, and we each had connection charms that could allow us to always find each other. After Rowan's disappearance, we'd bought them. Now, they were going to come in handy.

"We will send a transport mage with Ana to retrieve the buggy," Hedy said. "After that, she can get to know the organization a bit better. See that this would be a good place to work. Once you have the cure, you can do the same, Bree. Then we can talk more about terms of employment."

"All right," I said, even though I wasn't sure if I meant it. I couldn't think of anything past getting the cure and getting our buggy back.

Cade stepped forward, his gaze on me. "We should get started."

I shivered. Time alone with him?

Oh boy.

~

Caro, the terrifying water woman whom I actually kinda liked, met us as soon as we left the little library.

"Here!" She thrust plastic bags into each of our hands. "You smell like dead fish. I thought you might want these."

Normally, I'd take 'you smell like dead fish' to be an insult, but not coming from Caro. I looked in the bag, seeing black jeans, a black T-shirt, and leather jacket. Not my usual fight wear, but better than being covered in Lithica poison.

"Thanks," I said. "That's really...nice."

I was slightly at a loss. Taken aback by her kindness. It'd just been us for so long that this kind of thing was weird.

Don't be lured in by her kindness.

"I'll let you change," Cade said. "Then we can go."

"All right."

Caro showed Ana and I to a bathroom that looked like it'd been in the castle for centuries. Even the toilet was made of stone.

"Don't worry. It does flush." Caro stopped at the door. "And I know this place is weird at first, but I really think you'll like it here."

She went to leave, but I said, "Hang on."

"Yeah?"

"Who is Cade? *What* is Cade?" He had magic I'd never seen before.

"He's Belatucadros. The Celtic god of war." She grinned. "Crazy, right?"

A record scratch sounded inside my head. "Wait, what? A god?"

His power *had* been nuts.

"Yeah. He's one of the earth-walking gods. They're rare."

"What are they?" I asked. "Does that mean he's immortal? Like, ancient?"

Had I been eyeballing a dude old enough to be my grandfather eight hundred times removed? *Ew.*

"No. He's in his twenties, I think. He's a reincarnate. The godly power passes to the souls of those who are worthy. It's what allows him to walk the earth—because he's mortal. Yet he has the magical power of a god. Here at the Undercover Protectorate, he does the most dangerous jobs, and only on his terms."

"So he's not the boss?" Ana asked. "You all seemed to listen to him."

"Well, yeah. He's the best fighter here, and we like winning. So we listen to him. He leads the most dangerous operations, normally. Picks and chooses what he wants to do."

And he wanted to help me.

Hmmmm.

I stocked that away for later.

"Thanks, Caro."

She saluted. "No problem. Good luck with this cure. We'd really like to have you on the Paranormal Investigative Team."

"The PITs?"

She grinned widely. "Yep! Training is a bitch, but it's worth it in the end."

She departed, leaving just me and Ana.

"Is she for real? She's so...nice. Yet badass." I quickly tugged on the new clothes, my chest aching from the Lithica poison. The pain was steadier now—always present. But sometimes it seemed to flare.

I tossed the old ones in the trash, then tucked the pain potion that Hedy had given me into an inner pocket of the jacket, along with the wadded up bandana that held the potion bomb shards. At least they couldn't poke through the sturdy bandana.

"I think she might be." Ana frowned. "This place is weird."

"Yeah." Not quite the hardscrabble existence we were used to. Challenging, probably. But not the bullshit of scavenging for a living in an outlaw town full of criminals.

Not that I had time to worry about it now. I gave Ana a quick hug. "Be careful, okay? I'll be in touch. We've got our connection charms"—which, thankfully, we hadn't bought from Ricketts —"so I'll come find you when I'm done."

"If you're not back in three days, I'm coming for you."

I grinned and fist bumped her. "Deal."

"You gonna be okay with Cade? Because, meeeeow. And a god to boot."

I punched her in the shoulder.

"But seriously," she said. "He's a fox, and he's got eyes for you. I caught him looking at you a few times. Like he was perplexed and yet wants you at the same time."

I liked that even though I shouldn't. "We can't trust him."

"Maybe. I'd still climb him like a tree." She poked me in the chest. "But he looks at you. And he's got that scary sexy thing going on. Who doesn't like that?"

"Too scary. We can kick the ass of almost any guy who comes at us. Except him. *The god.*" Which I both loved and loathed. But it was too dangerous. "Anyway. Moot point. I'm off to find Ricketts, or we're going to turn into stone. You get the buggy, so we can start over after this."

Her gaze turned serious. Joking about hot guys only got us so far when the straights were this dire. "I'll take care of it."

She gave me another hug, then I left.

Walking away was weird—we usually faced life and all its dangers together. But this was the smartest way. A two prong attack increased our chances of success in the long run.

Cade waited for me in the hall. He held a small paper bag in his hand. "Ready?"

"Yeah. We're going to Magic's Bend, in Oregon. Do you have another transportation charm?" The things were super handy, but hard to come by.

"There's a portal here that will take us."

Wow. Those were also super rare. Only strong magic could keep portals running permanently. This place had everything. "Lead the way."

Cade handed me the paper bag. His fingertips brushed mine, and an electric frisson raced up my arm.

My gaze darted to the bag. "What's this?"

"I thought you might be hungry. And there's no telling what we'll face in pursuit of Ricketts."

My stomach grumbled, as if it could hear. I'd already had an exceptionally long day, and the food would be fuel. "Thanks."

As I dug into the bag and pulled out a sandwich, I followed Cade down the hall and through the main entryway. We passed several people, all of whom were covered in blood but looking surprisingly chipper. Until they saw me. Then their gazes turned suspicious.

I shot them challenging looks, my cheek full of sandwich like a lopsided hamster. *Like what you see?*

Not the best first impression, but I had to work with what I had.

"Why do people look at me like I'm going to steal the silver?" I asked.

"You're new. Everyone's safety relies upon everyone else. So when new people arrive, the armor of this place is weakened until that person proves loyal."

"But you guys trust us enough to bring us here?"

"We wouldn't bring you here otherwise. But it's the bosses who make the decisions, not the foot soldiers. So they're a little suspicious. You just have to prove it, and everyone will be okay with you. But there's an adjustment period."

Fair enough, though I didn't like it.

I followed Cade out the main door and around the castle to the side lawn, which stretched for acres before terminating at the forest. A stone circle sat in the distance, close to the seaside cliffs that fell into the crashing waves.

"Come on." He started down a path that cut across the grass. "The portals are in the forest."

We started down the path toward the trees.

"Who are we going to see in Magic's Bend?" Cade asked.

"My friends. They're Seekers. I have shards of the potion bomb, and they'll be able to use their magic to find Ricketts, who made it." *Lie.* They weren't really Seekers. They were Fire-Souls, a deadly species that could find anything using their dragon sense.

But I wasn't going to spill those beans to Cade, since it could totally get Cass, Del, and Nix into trouble.

"They must be powerful. We've had no luck finding him with Seekers."

"They are." And I prayed to fate they could give us a lead.

As we neared the trees, magic prickled against my skin, strong and fierce. I stepped between the trunks, spotting glowing lights floating amongst the green leaves. Green moss glowed under the little lights, and the trees were like gnarled old men, their branches twisted and bent.

My soul sighed, happy to be here. It was the most beautiful place. Haunted and magical at the same time.

"What are the lights?" I asked.

"Fairy lights. This was once an enchanted Fae grove, with a portal to their land. It's been sealed, however. Long ago."

"Wow."

He led me down the winding path. A river burbled somewhere nearby, but I couldn't see it. Eventually, we reached a clearing with three portals. They glowed in the dark night, one blue, one white, and one a faded gray.

I pointed to the gray one. "The Fae portal?"

"Yes."

"Why'd it close?"

"I don't know. It's been that way for centuries."

Cade pointed to the blue portal. "This one will take you to Edinburgh. The other, to Magic's Bend."

"Edinburgh?"

"Closest city with a magical community and great bars." His

lips tugged up at the corner. "The members of the Protectorate are big fans of the bars."

That didn't sound so bad.

I stepped toward the white portal, about to step through to Magic's Bend, the largest magical city in the world. It was an amazing place that humans had no idea existed.

Cade touched my arm. "I'll go first."

"I can handle it."

He smiled and stepped through, no doubt to scout the area for danger. I followed, letting the ether suck me through space, all the way from Scotland to Oregon.

I stepped out into an alley that smelled of burnt magic and pee. I crinkled my nose and went toward the main street, where Cade stood.

It was dark, shortly after 6:00 a.m., and the street was empty save for a few cars. On either side of the road sat pretty Victorian buildings three stories tall, each painted a different color. The first floors were all bars or restaurants. Looked pretty nice, though I hadn't been to this part of Magic's Bend before.

"Where are we?" I asked.

"This is the Historic District."

"Party district, is more like." No wonder that alley had smelled like pee.

"Hit the nail on the head."

A taxi drove by, and he flagged it down. We climbed into the glittering purple car and sat on seats of pink leather.

A pixie with green hair turned around. "Where ya off to?"

"Factory Row. A shop called Ancient Magic," I said.

The car peeled away from the curb.

"Ancient Magic?" Cade asked.

"Yep. My friends—" Were they really friends? I hadn't seen them in five years. Hopefully they weren't counting. "Um, my friends are treasure hunters. They find enchanted artifacts and sell the magic inside."

"Isn't it illegal to take antiquities from archaeological sites?"

I nodded. "They only take the artifacts with the most degraded magic." Over time, magic decayed. "They choose the pieces that are about to explode and remove the magic. That's what they sell. Then they return the original artifact to the archaeological site."

"Brilliant." Cade nodded. "That keeps them on the right side of the law, and they make a tidy profit."

"Exactly."

The taxi turned onto Factory Row, a street on the edge of town that housed all the old factories from the eighteenth and nineteenth centuries. It'd been converted into a trendy part of town with apartments and antique shops.

We drove by Potions & Pastilles, a coffee shop/bar that I'd been to a few times before. The lights glowed from within, and a dark-haired guy worked behind the counter, getting set up for the day. Connor, I thought his name was, but it'd been a while.

"Here!" I pointed to the spot where their shop, Ancient Magic, sat.

"Bit early for shopping." The driver pulled over.

"I know the owners." I reached into my pocket for my little wallet, but Cade handed over a wad of bills. "Thanks."

He nodded, and we got out of the car. It pulled off into the gloaming. I hurried onto the sidewalk, drawn by the golden light gleaming from the windows of Ancient Magic.

The owners—Cass, Del, and Nix—lived above the shop, but if the lights were on inside Ancient Magic, maybe I'd get lucky. Since my alternative was tossing pebbles at their windows above, I was hoping for lucky.

The wide glass windows revealed a red-headed figure behind the desk, fussing with something on the shelves.

"That's Cass." I stepped up to the door and tried it.

It gave way, and I stepped inside, Cade behind me.

Cass turned, her red hair swinging around the shoulders of

her brown leather jacket. She clutched a bronze figurine, and her eyes widened at the sight of me.

"Bree?" She stepped out from behind the counter. "It's been ages."

"Hi!" I waved, slightly awkwardly, and stepped farther into the shop. "You're here early."

She glanced at the artifact as if she'd forgotten she was holding it, and set it on the counter. "We're having trouble with this artifact. Nix can't get the magic out, and it's about to blow. We need to get it out of here."

"Oh, shit." I stepped backward.

"Don't worry—the artifact has a day, at least. So we have a few minutes. Live dangerously, right?" She stepped closer. She wore jeans and tall leather boots, completing her Indiana Jones/Lara Croft hybrid look. She was one of the most badass supernaturals out there, and was someone I'd always respected. "But why are you here? Not that it's not great to see you. I'd just hoped we'd have seen you more in the last five years."

"Yeah, sorry about that." I was keenly aware of Cade at my side, his ears tuned to pick up every bit of the conversation. "We were busy."

"Hmmm. If you'd needed help…" She trailed off when I stiffened.

Though I appreciated the offer, Ana and I liked to take care of ourselves. Cass understood that kind of pride.

Even though we were now at the end of our line.

"What can I do for you, then?" Cass asked.

"We need help finding something."

"Yeah, sure, of course." She stepped closer, then pulled up short, raising her palms. "Whoa. Hello power."

I glanced up at Cade. "Get your magical signature under control, man."

Magical signatures could be controlled by powerful supernaturals. Cade definitely counted. So why was he blasting his at

Cass? Did he sense how powerful she was, too? She was keeping hers on the down low, from what I could tell.

"Um, not him," Cass said. "Though I can tell he's holding on to some serious firepower. It's you, Bree. You've got some mad power going on."

"Me?" My signature had always been pretty normal.

"Yeah." Her gaze darted to Cade, then went blank. As if she realized that maybe I didn't want to talk about it in front of him. As a FireSoul, one who shared a soul with a dragon, Cass knew all too well what it was like to hide your power. She'd been hiding for years. She was trying to protect me. "Anyway, what kind of help do you need? And who is your big pal here?"

"I'm Cade." He stepped forward and held out his hand.

"Cade." Cass shot him an appraising glance, like she was trying to figure him out. "Hang on. You're Belatucadros!"

"Aye. But would you introduce yourself with that mouthful?"

I liked that he didn't parade around with his godly name. He let his actions speak, not his title.

She laughed. "Fair enough, god of war." She shook his hand, then turned to me. "Spill."

"We need your help to track someone. We have something they used," I said.

"Of course."

I tugged the bandana out of my pocket and held it out. "Careful. The shards may have poison on them."

Cass took it, then opened it and peered at the contents. "Do you know anything else about this person?"

"Yes," I said. "We're looking for the man who made it. A Blood Sorcerer named Ricketts. But it was deployed by another man. He's dead."

"All right." She closed her eyes, no doubt calling on her dragon sense.

Because she was so powerful, I couldn't feel a hint of her magic. She'd probably practiced long and hard to conceal something that strong. Her power came directly from dragons. Since the magical beasts were so covetous, they were able to find anything of value. FireSouls had inherited that gift.

A pretty valuable power, if you asked me.

A moment later, her eyes popped open. "Ricketts is somewhere in Europe. If I were closer, I could give you a more precise location. But the man who deployed it—he's dead, you said?"

"Yeah," I said.

"Well, his ashes or body are nearby." She pulled out her phone and tapped some buttons, then held it out to me. "I think he's in this house. I can feel it really strongly since he's so close."

I peered at the satellite image on Google maps. A modern mansion sat on a cliff by the sea. Several large, black SUVs sat in the drive. Exactly the kind of cars you'd think a mobster's goons would drive. "That looks like a frat house for mob muscle."

Cade nodded sharply. "That would make sense. We have reports that he keeps mercenaries on staff in different locations. Having his American base in Magic's Bend is logical."

It was the largest magical city in the world and had a massive airport for reaching headquarters in Europe, so yeah, that made sense.

"Even if he's not there, I bet there's a lead there," I said.

Cass nodded. "Try that out. If it doesn't work, I'll be done with this artifact in a couple days. I could help you locate Ricketts in Europe."

"Thank you." I definitely wanted to get started with this lead, but the backup option was nice.

"Anytime. Really." She handed the glass shards back to me, questions in her eyes.

"I'll meet you on the street okay, Cade?" I shot him a glance. I wanted just a moment alone with her. She'd been the closest thing to a friend outside of my sister that I'd ever had, and that was really laughable, considering that I'd barely known her.

He gave Cass a searching look, then nodded. "Good to meet you, Cass."

I watched him walk out, then turned to Cass.

"You're stronger than you were," she said. "Much stronger. And five years ago, when I met you, you were no one to be trifled with. But now it's a bit crazy."

"I know. I'm not sure what it is. I'm an Unknown. And my power has been going wild lately. Any control I once had is gone." Unknowns often manifested their true powers later in life. Was that what was happening to me?

For the first time ever, I found myself spilling my guts. But I could trust Cass, because she knew what it was like to hide. And she'd keep my secret. Just like I'd kept hers.

I trusted very few people in this world—less than I could count on one hand—and she was one of them. Even if my pride was too big to accept more help than absolutely necessary.

"Don't let anyone know what you are." Her gaze was serious. "I know what that life is like. I found my way out—to happiness and honesty—but hiding is what kept me alive for the first twenty-five years."

"That's exactly what my mother told me to do. She was a seer, and she prophesied that someone would hunt me because of what I am. Except, I don't even know what I am exactly. Just that I might be changing."

She nodded. "Keep hiding. Try to get a handle on your magic. You must. And learn to control your signature. That will save you."

I nodded, grateful for the advice. Cass was about seven years older than me and had lived a life that was just as hard and full of secrets. She knew what was up.

"I don't know how well you know Cade," she said. "So I'm sorry if I blew your cover. I was just so shocked. It's almost impossible for non-FireSouls to increase their magical power. And you aren't a FireSoul. I'd feel it if you were."

I hadn't ever wanted to be—FireSouls were never Unknowns —but answers would be nice. "It's cool. I appreciate the help."

"Come back to see us again. Nix and Del would be happy to see you. And if you need us, we'll help. Like you helped us."

"Thanks. Really." I took one last glance at her face, this almost-friend who could possibly be more if I weren't so damned scared of getting close to people, then turned for the door.

"Hang on," she said. "I don't see a car out in the street. Did you take a cab? Where's your crazy truck?"

I turned. "Temporarily out of commission."

Cass grinned. "You'll need a ride out to the target's house, then. I bet Nix would let you borrow her new baby."

From what little I knew, Cass's sister Nix loved cars. "Really? I haven't spoken to you guys in five years, and she'd do that?"

"You helped her a lot. And you're going to like this car."

"What is it?"

"A version of your truck. Nix loved yours so much she built a smaller one for herself. It'll probably come in handy getting to the target's house. Dollars to donuts there are protection charms around the property."

Excitement thrummed in my veins. I was always most comfortable fighting from a vehicle, and this would come in handy. "Thanks."

Cass nodded and pressed a finger to the golden charm at her throat. Magic thrummed in the air. "Nix? You'll never guess who is here. Bree Blackwood. Can she borrow your truck?"

"Bree?" Nix's voice spiked with excitement. "Heck yeah. There are spare keys in the desk, and it's parked in the alley. Tell her she should come by more."

"Thanks, Nix," I said, directing my voice toward Cass's communications charm. Ana and I really needed to get some of those.

"No problem," Nix said. "Good luck with whatever you're after. And Cass, I'll see you in twenty?"

"Yeah, I've got the artifact and I'm coming." Cass hung up on the comms charm and looked at me. "Let's get you in this car, then I've got to get this damned artifact away from civilization while we try to sort out the magic."

"Thanks again." I smiled at her, my heart warmed.

Had Ana and I done the wrong things, sticking so close to ourselves all these years? I hadn't realized that Cass and Nix had liked us so much. Maybe we'd given up something good.

Maybe.

CHAPTER FOUR

Nix's car turned out to be a modified Hummer with fighting platforms on the front and back. No spikes on the sides, but massive tires gave the thing good clearance, and the engine was nothing to be trifled with.

I waved goodbye to Cass and pulled out of the alley, Cade at my side.

"You like your cars," he said.

"Depends." I turned off of Factory Row and headed out of town. "I like cars that help me fight. Beasts like this do that."

He grinned, then looked at his phone, where he had the map. Cass had marked the house for us. "Go left up here."

I turned at his directions, heading toward the forests that surrounded Magic's Bend. Thirty minutes later, we neared our target. The woods had thickened, and the street had narrowed.

"You can tell they're up to no good just by their location," I muttered. We were well away from any of the perks of town. There weren't even any other houses out here.

"Turn here." Cade pointed to an even narrower road that cut through giant, twisted trees.

I turned onto the gravel lane, the car easily tackling the gravel road. "It's like we're headed into the Big Bad Wolf's forest."

"Dark magic can warp a place." Cade leaned forward, studying the terrain. "Two hundred yards ahead."

I peered through the trees, unable to see the house. It was darker here, unnaturally so. But magic sparked on the air, growing stronger. Like most protection charms, it stung the skin. Tiny bee stings that said *get the hell out of here.*

I pressed my foot to the gas, speeding up. Trees closed in. Magic vibrated on the air.

Then the ground began to rumble, rough and low. Moving earth.

I kicked into action, instinct born of years fighting in the desert. "Take the wheel!"

I hopped out of the seat, launching myself onto the front platform without waiting to see if Cade followed my orders. He was a smart guy. He'd figure it out.

Just as I landed on the small metal platform, one of the trees ahead burst out of the ground.

Ha! I'd known something was about to pop out.

Death Valley threw a lot of things at us, and monsters made of the terrain were common.

The massive tree vibrated with magic as it morphed into a giant boar made of wood and bark. Pine needles for hair stuck out wildly, and the eyes were gaping black pits.

Always the gaping black pits with these monsters.

I grinned, kinda liking it. Made it easier to destroy them if I didn't have to look into their eyes. They weren't real, but it was easy to pretend they were.

Cade kept the car on the lane as I powered up my magic and aimed for the boar that charged us. It was bigger than the car, its wooden hooves pounding the earth and its great tusks ready to flip the vehicle onto its back.

I sucked in a deep breath, then hurled my magic at the boar. It shot out of me like a deflating balloon.

Shit!

Totally unpredictable these days.

A deep growl rumbled from the boar's chest as the beast thundered toward us, kicking up massive clods of earth. It was only twenty yards away now.

One shot.

I tried to grab the magic tumbling around inside my chest, a wild thing that refused to cooperate. Finally, I nabbed it, imagining a giant sonic boom and heaving it toward the monster.

It cracked on the air and bowled the beast over, slamming into the surrounding trees and uprooting two of them. The boar was now twigs.

I winced.

Slight overkill.

"Faster!" I shouted to Cade as I crouched on the platform and held on to the railing. Ana would *not* be pleased by my lack of safety harness. I didn't know if we could outrun any of the protection charms, but we could sure as heck try.

"Aye!" Cade shouted.

The vehicle shot forward, racing past trees. Wind tore at my hair as I scanned the forest, searching for threats. The way the magic prickled on the air, there was something waiting for us.

When the ground ahead shifted, like something slithered under the leaves, I drew my sword and shield from the ether. They were familiar and comforting in my hands, but I'd really have to watch my balance without my harness.

"Something up ahead!" I shouted. "Be wary."

A massive black snake burst from the ground ahead of us, to the right of the road, scales gleaming black in the light. Diamond eyes flared bright in its head.

Nothing this big could be natural—not in Oregon. And not with diamond eyes. Magic, then. Not living.

Whew.

Less on my conscience this way.

I shifted, ready for it.

The creature struck, fast as lightning, coming straight for me. Fangs glinted in its mouth. I raised my shield to block and swung my sword, going for the neck.

My sword sliced through the creature's neck, and the head flew off. Sparkling gray blood sprayed from the neck, splattering my shield and sizzling.

Whoa. Definitely not blood.

The massive body thudded to the ground.

"Left!" Cade shouted.

I spun, catching sight of a second snake coming from the other side of the vehicle. I lunged for it. *Too late for the sword.* I crouched low, raising my shield as it struck. The head slammed into my shield, driving me backwards. I barely maintained my footing, my arm aching from the blow.

When I lowered my shield, the snake was rallying for a second hit. One of its foot-long fangs was broken, no doubt from its collision with my shield.

The snake's diamond gaze darted between me and Cade.

"Shield!" I shouted, just as the snake struck out at Cade.

His magic surged on the air as he conjured his shield on the arm that faced the snake. It appeared just as the beast neared him.

I lunged, slicing the snake's neck with my blade. The silvery gray blood sprayed again, sizzling as it struck Cade's shield and the side of the car. I ducked, barely avoiding the spray, as Cade pressed his foot to the gas and the vehicle sped forward.

"Good job," he shouted.

"You too!" I turned for the front of the truck, searching for more protection charms.

Instead, pain flared in my chest like an explosion of acid, making me gasp and double over. I barely kept my footing on the platform. The Lithica poison was really hitting me now. I sucked in ragged breaths, trying to get it together.

"Are you all right?" Cade shouted.

"Fine." I bit out the words, straightening as the pain faded to a dull roar. Still there, but not incapacitating. These flare-ups were getting worse and worse.

Ahead of us, there was a massive mansion, sitting on the cliff. It gleamed with metal and glass, a modern construction that looked like a rectangular spaceship. If that kind of thing even existed.

Two men stood on the porch, magic glowing around them like a threat.

"Looks like we lost the element of surprise!" I shouted. "Let's ditch the car!"

I really didn't want to hurt it more than we already had. I'd definitely be repairing those burns in the paint from the snake's weird blood—I didn't want to actually total the whole car.

Cade slowed the vehicle about twenty yards from the house. Before he could stop, I leapt off the platform, running full out for the mages, shield and sword raised.

One looked just like the dead mage who'd nailed me with the poison—his twin brother. Unlike the mage who had hit me with the potion bomb and had worn a hideous blue leather jacket, this one wore a sleek three-piece suit. The other was a hulking blond man wearing a horrible gold track suit.

"Where is Ricketts?" I demanded as I neared. Maybe we'd get lucky and they'd tell us.

"Hell if we're telling you." The mage's brother flung out his hand. An electrical whip snapped through the air, coming right for me.

Right. So that had failed.

I raised my shield. The electric whip cracked off the metal. The shock sent vibrations up my arm, but it didn't electrocute me. The shield was backed by rubber—I wasn't a total newb.

But Cade needed to park the car and get here ASAP, because magic was starting to glow around Goldie. He was about to get into the action, and I didn't want to fight off two.

"Your brother hit me with the Lithica poison," I shouted. "That means Ricketts *wants* me to come to him. Where is he?"

"Like I can trust you." He struck again, this time going low.

I barely managed to shield myself in time. The whip cracked against the metal.

The man next to him growled, his magic glowing even stronger, a bright light that flared as he grew larger. His muscles popped, and he shot up four feet in height—like some transformer doll or the Hulk.

Except that he was an unfortunate peachy color and looked like a twelve-foot-tall 'roided up body builder. Cade's footsteps thundered behind me as he approached. Out of the corner of my eye, I saw him shift into a *massive* wolf, then lunge for the giant.

Holy crap.

He was no ordinary Shifter. Apparently the god thing gave him some extra juice, because he was four times the size of a normal wolf.

I left him to it, raising my blade as the mage across from me powered up his magic. Fortunately, he needed a few seconds between blasts.

"Seriously, man," I shouted. "I need to know where Ricketts is. The potion proves he wants to see me."

"Tony didn't mention 'nothin about no Lithica potion." He snapped out with his whip, which I barely avoided. "You think we're idiots? We got protocol, lady! Ricketts keeps his location a secret. Lotta people want him dead, but none of us squeal on him. That's the *point!* If you have to nail someone with the Lithica curse, only *you* deliver Ricketts's location."

Dang, he was red in the face. Pretty pissed, really.

And he was *not* gonna give up the location of Ricketts. I knew what commitment looked like, and this guy had it. That meant we had to search the house.

The growls and shrieks from nearby indicated that Cade was taking care of his goon, so I just had to handle mine.

I lunged for him just as he struck out with his electrical whip. I blocked it, then swung my sword. He danced back, faster than I could see.

"Super speed, too." He grinned evilly, raising his hand again. "I am going to fuck you up. Rip out your intestines and turn them into a bow."

Right, then. Super speed plus electrical whip equaled *this was not a sword fight.*

I stashed my sword in the ether, then flung out my hand, aiming a moderate sized sonic boom at him. I'd just knock him unconscious and start searching the house.

It exploded out of me like a freight train, bowling him over and destroying half of the house in a shower of glass and metal.

Shit.

I stumbled back, muscles suddenly weak. I'd blown all my magic in one go. And that dude was definitely dead.

Okay, that had been bad. I looked over in time to see Cade tear the throat out of the big man and leap off of him. Blood and gore dripped down his muzzle. He was as tall as me in this form, and a good two or three hundred pounds heavier.

I swallowed hard. "Hey, Cade."

Please don't eat me.

I'd used up all my magic—unintentionally—and did not want to get eaten as a result.

Silver light swirled around him, and he transformed back to human, dressed and with no blood coating his face. His gaze traveled over the half destroyed house.

"It's hard to search a house when it's rubble," he said.

"I know." But I *really* didn't want to explain how I lost control. "You're half Shifter?"

"No. Wolves were important to the Celts. Warrior dogs. It's part of my god power. I don't qualify as a Shifter and wouldn't be welcome at Glencarrough."

Glencarrough was the Alpha Council's secretive headquarters. If they knew what an ally Cade could be, I'd bet they'd invite him in.

He looked like he was about to ask me about the catastrophe that I'd caused, so I jumped in. "Cool. Let's go check the house."

I hurried toward the front door. It'd once been a double door, but only one was left. The whole right side of the house was now rubble.

Please let their rooms be on the left.

I yanked open the remaining door and hurried into a massive living room that was half destroyed.

Cade followed. "We'll talk about this later."

Not if I can help it. "Can't wait."

All the couches were gone, but an urn sat on the coffee table. "There's the mage."

"Aye. Brother must have brought him back."

I winced, guilt streaking through me over the death of two brothers. They'd been evil assholes out to kill me, but still...

Ignoring the urn, I hurried toward the door on the left. A quick survey showed a closet full of three-piece suits. "It's the brother's room."

Cade looked up from where he'd been looking into the small garbage bin. "Trash is full of receipts from Venice. Dated last month."

"Hmmm. That's in Europe." I left the room, going to the next. The closet in this one revealed a collection of giant track suits. "Strike out."

"Let's look anyway."

We found more receipts from Venice from six weeks ago.

"Looks like more than a coincidence," I said.

"Here's hoping for three."

We left the room and found the final bedroom on the upper floor. The closet contained colorful leather jackets. Red, orange, blue. *Bingo*. Thank fates I hadn't destroyed this room. "This is his room."

I hurried to the desk, while Cade grabbed the little garbage bin. I riffled through papers for a few moments while he searched.

"Nothing in here," he said.

"That's because he hasn't thrown them out yet." I held up a handful of receipts. "Also Venice. Dated last week."

"Then none of them were traveling together."

"Not a vacation. They were going to get their orders. And it seems that Ricketts runs an organized operation. They saved their receipts so they could submit them for reimbursement."

Cade nodded. "Good work."

"Stupid trail, though." But I grinned, grateful for the slip up. We needed all the help we could get. "This place was protected, but not well enough."

"Not from us." Cade smiled warmly at me, the corners of his beautiful eyes crinkling. Wind swept his dark hair off his face and pressed his sweater to his muscular chest. Butterflies started dancing in my stomach. "We make a good team."

Warmth glowed in my chest, joining the butterflies down below.

A connection. We definitely had one. And we'd done this together.

Oooohkay, whoa, Nelly.

Feeling warm fuzzies about a dude was the first step toward a...relationship. Yikes.

Relationships were a bad idea. They required trust. I was not good at that, and I couldn't afford it anyway—not with the way my magic was going haywire lately.

If they knew what I really was? Ana and I would be out on our asses—no more help from the Undercover Protectorate. And I wanted to be damned sure I'd get my hands on that cure before we parted ways.

"Let's get out of here," I said. "I bet more than three people lived in a house this big. The others might be back soon."

"Good plan."

We hurried out of the house, headed back toward Nix's car. Exhaustion pulled at me as I climbed into the passenger seat. Cade had the keys, and I was on shaky legs already. He could drive. I'd used up all my magic and hadn't actually slept in what felt like days. We'd gone straight from Death Valley to this.

Cade turned the car on and pulled away from the house. "I have an underworld contact in Venice. If Ricketts is there, she'll probably know about them."

"Good. Another lead."

"It'll be evening in Scotland. We'll sleep tonight and start in the morning."

As much as I wanted to start hunting the cure immediately, I desperately needed a bit of sleep. And my magic was totally out. It'd take a while to recoup all that I'd blown. "All right."

After a few moments, Cade broke the silence. "Did you mean to destroy the house?"

I wanted to say yes—not to admit to my wonky magic—but there was literally no way I could. No one would destroy the house they wanted to search. "Sometimes I put a little too much juice on my magic."

"Hmmm." His gaze turned to my face, thoughtful. "And your friend said that your magic is stronger."

Shit. He had been listening. But I couldn't let him realize that's what was happening to me. That I was maybe changing from an Unknown into....what? "I wore a magic repressing charm when I saw her last."

Please buy that.

Those things did technically exist, though I'd never gotten my hands on one.

LINSEY HALL

"Really?" He sounded skeptical.

"Yep."

"Either way, your lack of control could be a problem in Venice."

No kidding. My magic was all about blowing stuff up, and everywhere I looked, there were either people or valuable historic buildings.

Not the place for me.

"I'll just stick to my weapons. I can handle anything with those."

The corner of his mouth tugged up. "I believe that. You're damned skilled." He drove down Factory Row and parked the truck in the alley. "I think I can probably get you a charm that will help you control your magic. It's a temporary fix because the charm's magic fades. You'll have to train hard to get your magic under control, but this could help in the meantime."

"Really?" That'd be handy.

"Aye. There's an armory at the Protectorate. They can make one. It'll take the night, but they'll do it."

"For the god of war."

"Aye. But for any member who needs it."

"Is that me?"

"If you complete your training." He turned off the car and met my gaze. "Which I hope you will."

"Caro said it can be a real bitch."

He grinned. "Of course. That's how you join the most elite secret organization in the world."

"I'd expect nothing less."

CHAPTER FIVE

We arrived at the portal in the enchanted forest right as dusk was falling. We hadn't spoken much on the cab ride back to the portal in Magic's Bend, but I'd felt Cade's presence intensely.

I was definitely interested. And he might've even returned the sentiment.

Which just made me more nervous.

And more curious.

We set off toward the castle in silence. The path back through the woods was lit by the fairy lights, giving the place a romantic feel, which I did my damnedest to ignore.

At the edge of the forest, Cade spoke. "I'll submit a request to the armory for your charm. If they start immediately, it should be done by morning. Once we have it, we'll head to Venice."

"How will we get there?" I hoped he had a transport charm. I didn't want to spend hours on a plane. Not with this deadline.

He dug into the pocket of his battered leather jacket and withdrew a black stone.

Jackpot.

"How are you getting so many of those?" They were super rare because they were so hard to make.

"I have a wizard contact that I pay well."

"Handy."

"Very."

We walked up the path toward the castle. I called upon the connection charm that I had with my sister, feeling a tug toward the low buildings on the other side of the castle, near the wall.

I pointed to them. "What are those?"

"The stables. They're now used as garages and storage. If your sister recovered your vehicle, it'll be in there."

"She's in there, too, if the buggy is." Probably working on it. "I'm going to go check it out."

"All right. If she's there, Caro will have shown her around a bit. If you need anything, there's a small office immediately to the right of the main foyer. They can help you."

"You're just going to let me wander around unsupervised?"

"Aye. That's part of the trust thing I mentioned."

This was their home, technically. And probably full of all kinds of magic that I could nick.

We weren't thieves. We earned our livings honestly. But the fact that they would trust us?

Kinda cool, even though I hated to admit it.

Also maybe a little stupid. But that didn't detract from the cool factor.

"How do you know you can trust us, though?"

"Our potential members are selected very carefully. It's not easy to get an invitation. It's an honor really. But once you've been chosen, it's up to you to earn your place with your skill in training."

"How are we chosen? You didn't even interview us."

"*That* is a secret." He grinned. He was a devastatingly handsome man who looked like he fit right into the Scottish Highlands. "And if I told you, I'd have to kill you."

"All right, then." I couldn't help my smile even as I swore I'd figure out how we'd been chosen.

"I'm off to the armory. I'll see you in the morning at six, in the entry hall. We'll get started early."

"Thanks."

He nodded. "Thank *you*. We've wanted to catch Ricketts for a long time."

As he walked away, I watched his very attractive backside stride off into the night.

Nope! I spun around

Eyes on the prize, Bree. And my prize wasn't going to have anything to do with Cade's butt. My prize was going to be the cure for the Lithica poison and getting Ricketts off my back. As an added bonus, we'd be able to repair the buggy.

This would all work out.

Somehow.

I turned down the path toward the stables. The path and grounds were empty at this hour, probably because everyone was eating dinner. It was a beautiful evening, with the sun low near the mountains and the breeze light. Wildflowers rustled, and the castle rose tall in the distance. It was surreal to be walking around such a beautiful place.

I liked it. The whole place felt magical. Not the everyday kind of magic that I lived with, but the kind that I'd always associated with castles and history. Fairytale magic.

And I was here.

Agony exploded in my chest. I gasped and stumbled, barely keeping to my feet. My head swam as I sucked in shallow breathes, trying to get control of it.

Oh, fates.

This was getting bad.

Just the idea of the Lithica poisoning turning my insides to stone made me cringe. I hoped Ana wasn't feeling the same thing.

By the time I neared the stables, I could hear Ana cursing within. I pulled open the heavy door and stepped into the

71

warmth, breathing in deeply the scent of engine oil. It overlaid the smell of hay and horses that still lingered. Nice.

"Hey!" Ana stepped out from behind the buggy, which looked like a burned-out mess.

"Oh hell! What happened to the buggy?" I frowned and inspected it.

"Just like you thought. Ricketts sent more men, who lit it up with fireballs. Caro, Ali, and Haris helped me drive them off before they could destroy the whole thing. Then a seriously powerful transport mage helped us get it back." She patted the hood and scrubbed a cloth over her face, getting rid of some of the grease on her cheek. "But I think it's mostly cosmetic. I can get it fixed up pretty soon."

"Really?"

"Yeah. This ol' boy isn't doing so bad." She patted the bumper, as if to prove it, but the thing fell off and crashed to the ground.

I winced. "Going to take some work."

"No kidding." She nudged the bumper with her foot. It broke in two.

Ouch.

But at least we had it back. "Caro, Ali, and Haris helped you fight them off?"

"Yep. Pretty cool of them."

Yeah. It'd been part of the deal for us staying here, true, but I was glad they'd done it. Any time someone stuck their neck out for me was cool.

"How'd it go with you?" Ana asked.

I explained the lead.

"That sounds promising." She rubbed her chest. "Because I'm really starting to feel it. I took the potion a few hours ago. It helped a bit."

"I think I'll take mine soon." I fingered the pain potion in my pocket, not yet ready to take it. "But I feel good about this lead.

And now that you have the buggy and can fix it up, things are looking hopeful for when we leave here."

"Yeah. Leave." Her expression was torn.

"You don't want to?"

"No, I do. Totally. We're best on our own. But today didn't suck, Bree. Caro showed me around, and it's beautiful. And some people—okay, a lot—shot me suspicious looks. But Caro is really cool. And so are Ali and Haris. This place has potential."

"Let's just get the cure and get Ricketts off our backs first."

"Solid plan." Ana walked toward a wide table set up against the wall and picked up a plate of sandwiches. She turned and offered it to me. "Hungry?"

My stomach growled. "Heck yeah. But where did these come from?"

"Ali brought them down."

I took one and bit in, sighing happily at the taste. This was high quality ham and cheese—not that crap we used to buy. I swallowed, then asked, "Ali, the same Djinn who helped with the car?"

"Yeah. He came to introduce himself better. You just missed him."

"And he brought food." I frowned. "So what did he want in return?"

Ana's brow scrunched. "Nothing, I don't think."

"Weird. He didn't hit on you?"

"No. Which is also weird."

"Huh." Someone had done something nice for nothing. *Does not compute.* "So he just came down to say hi?"

I couldn't wrap my freaking mind around it.

"Yeah. And he figured that since the lights were still on, I'd missed dinner."

I chomped on the sandwich, mulling the whole thing over. Then I shrugged. Some people were weird.

The door creaked open and I turned.

Caro poked her head in. "Hey! Want to come to the pub?"

"The pub?" I asked.

"Yeah. You know, place you drink." She made a drinking motion. "Everyone's going. It's Friday night. You should come."

"Us?" Ana asked.

"Yeah, dummy. You're part of the group now. Come on."

"We haven't even done training yet. Or officially accepted."

"You will. Training will kick your ass, but you'll be official soon enough. So come on."

I looked at Ana. Her slightly confused expression mirrored my own feelings. We were like freaking feral cats, not trusting that anyone would just want to...be nice.

It made me uncomfortable. But I was also weird. I'd seen TV —I knew that not everyone was like us. And Caro was so genuine.

"I'm pretty beat," I said. Oddly, regret winged in my chest. "And I have a big day tomorrow."

"Yeah, same," Ana said.

"It's only six fifteen," Caro said. "Come for an hour. Meet some people. If you're going to stick around, you'll want to know the others."

But we weren't going to stick around.

Except that the offer did sound really nice. Hanging out with other people. Friendly people.

I looked at Ana, noticing how torn she looked. She wanted to go, too, even though it was so weird for us.

"An hour," I said. "But then I need to rest up for tomorrow."

"Great!" Caro turned and left, shouting behind her. "Come on!"

"Okay, this is nuts." Ana scrubbed the rest of the grease off her face and grabbed half a sandwich. "But I'm kinda psyched. Is that weird?"

"We can just be normal for a little while," I said. We didn't party much, and it was tempting to just go have fun. Especially when I was worried about the poison.

We followed Caro outside. The two Djinn waited, kicking a hacky sack around.

"Are those two always playing?" I asked.

"Pretty much."

At the sound of our voices, the guys looked up and grinned.

"Hey!" Ali stepped forward. "Good to see you."

Haris grinned and waved.

Something about the guys made them feel familiar. Warm, almost.

It was weird.

I didn't want to like this place so much, or these people. But I did.

"Come on, this way." Caro led us down the path toward the enchanted forest.

"Where's the pub?" Ana asked.

"In Edinburgh. We'll take a portal," Ali said.

"Cool." I glanced at Caro. "So, you really like it here?"

"Love it." She gazed around the grounds, her eyes shining. "I was skeptical at first, too. I had a good thing going, working as a mercenary in Magic's Bend. But this is *way* better. And I hear they're really excited to have you on board. You must be important."

I laughed. "Doubtful."

"Dangerous, then," she said.

"Probably that." I looked at her. She'd changed out of her battle attire, which had been all black leather, into jeans and a black T-shirt. "But you're pretty deadly too. What are you?"

"Half water sprite, half demon."

"Ah," Ana said. "That's why you can shoot water that will cut straight through a person."

Caro wiggled her fingers. "Yep!"

We passed a man with tired eyes and flyaway blond hair. His

pale skin was creased with stress wrinkles, and his clothes looked like they could use a good wash.

"Hey, Stanley!" Caro said.

He just grunted, absentminded.

"Stanley's always been a bit in the clouds," Caro said. "Likes to wander the mountains most of the time."

"Not content in his work here?" I asked.

"I think he likes it, but he's a magical theorist. They spend a lot of time with their minds elsewhere."

A magical theorist? This place had everything.

We kept chatting as we walked down the path toward the forest. It was friendly. And nice.

Ali liked weird sports like frisbee golf and curling, while Haris was into computers. Caro just seemed cool in general, with a penchant for talking about old battles and music. Pretty bad music, but who was I to judge? My favorite song was "Mississippi Squirrel Revival."

Ana and I kept shooting each other bemused glances. We *knew* that people behaved like this, but we'd never experienced it. Death Valley Junction was full of criminals, so our social scene had been way different.

Like, nonexistent.

This kind of easy friendship and acceptance was…unusual.

Caro led us all through the pretty forest, down the path surrounded by gnarled old trees. The lights led the way, and little creatures skittered through the underbrush. Something with large eyes peered out at me.

"Terrier mouse," Caro said. "Cute and creepy at the same time. I've heard they'll grant wishes if you can catch them."

"No one's ever caught one, though," Ali said. "But there's loads of magical creatures in the forest. After the walls were built, it became a sanctuary for them."

"That's awesome." I'd always hated that magical creatures and non-magical creatures alike were threatened, with more becoming extinct every year as development grew. The fact that this was also a sanctuary was awesome.

Ugh, this place was so cool it was killing me.

We stopped in the clearing near the portals. Magic pulsed against my skin.

"Come on." Caro stepped through the portal.

I followed, gasping at the feel of the ether sucking me in. It was a short, whirlwind ride through space, then it spit me out in the middle of a bustling city street.

Magical signatures buffeted me from all directions.

Immediately, I pressed my back against the nearest wall, scouting my surroundings.

Beneath the golden street lamps, the street heaved with supernaturals of all species. Shifters, mages, fae, and even a few demons—who shouldn't actually be walking the earth. They all bustled down the sidewalk, splitting off into pubs and shops. Wings and tails and feathers were out in full force, and no one's magic was dampened.

Though I scouted for a threat, none came up.

This was just a hell of a lot of people out for a Friday night.

"Festival." Ali groaned. "I forgot."

"What's that?" Ana asked.

"The humans have a big culture festival in August. The city becomes a madhouse. About ten years ago, the supernaturals decided they should be partying just as hard. So now they hit the Grassmarket hard during festival time."

Caro caught sight of the confused look on my face and grinned. "The Grassmarket is what this neighborhood is called. It's the all-supernatural zone of Edinburgh. A powerful spell diverts humans from coming here."

"Cool." Slowly, I relaxed my fight stance and took in my surroundings.

The buildings were old and the street cobbled. To my left, a steep staircase led up through an alley, rising over a hundred feet.

"The Royal Mile is that way," Ali said. "Human zone." He leaned right and pointed up the main cobbled street. "The castle is there."

I leaned out and looked, catching sight of a hulking castle sitting on a craggy cliff over two hundred feet tall. Suddenly, bagpipes blared through the air, coming from the castle.

It was freaking amazing. There was *so much* here. Nothing like Death Valley.

"Very Scottish," Ana said.

"Wait till you have the Haggis." Caro grinned.

"I'll start with a drink." I looked around. "Which to the pub?"

"Right this way!" Caro darted out into the crowd of people and sailed along with them. I joined the masses, easily keeping sight of her platinum head.

She led us to a little pub called the Whisky and Warlock, ducking low to get in through the little door. I followed.

The interior was warm and welcoming. Little rooms branched out from the tiny entry, and we went left, heading into a room with a small bar and a low ceiling supported by beams that looked like tree trunks that had been painted black. A fire burned in the fireplace at the back, and supernaturals were crowded around little tables.

Despite the welcoming feel of the place, I kept my guard up.

Old habits died hard. For good reason, in this case.

The gleaming wooden bar was set up near the entrance. There was a trendy young woman at the counter filling pints and pouring Scotch.

I glanced at Ana. "Pretty cool, huh?"

"Yeah."

I didn't want to be impressed, but I was a country mouse at heart. A deadly country mouse, to be fair, but I'd spent most of my life in rural towns. The fact that this place was just a step away from the Protectorate's home base was amazing.

"Come on, I've got the first round." Caro led the way up to the bar.

I squeezed in next to her, leaning on the shining wooden surface and surveying my options. Golden bottles decorated the shelves behind the bartender. Lots of Scotch. But also a few colorful ones that called to me.

The bartender came over, wiping her hands on a white towel and smiling. "What'll it be, Caro?"

"Hey, Sophie. Three pints of Tennent's." Caro looked at me and Ana. "You?"

"Something sweet?" An umbrella would be ideal, but this didn't seem like the kind of place.

"A Pink Squirrel?" Sophie asked.

"Sounds perfect." I had no idea what that was, but I loved me a sweet or fruity cocktail and the sillier the name, the better. So Pink Squirrel fit the bill.

"I'll have a beer," Ana said.

Sophie nodded and went to fill the orders.

Caro pulled her wallet from her pocket. I pulled out mine, but Caro laid a hand on my arm. "I've got this one."

"No way," I said. "We can pay our own way."

At least for a few drinks. Literally down to what was in my wallet, basically. And maybe it was a bad idea to spend that money, but a tiny bit of fun for exactly one hour wouldn't hurt.

"You get the next round. And just put it on your tab."

"I have a tab?"

"Yeah, now that you work for the Protectorate. This is our place. Sophie runs a tab for each of us that is paid off automatically on payday."

Our place. I liked the sound of that. The bars back in Death Valley Junction had been the territory of grouchy old men. This was way better.

"Nice system." I accepted the Pink Squirrel with a smile. "Thanks."

Caro introduced us to Sophie and told her to set up an account. I shared a glance with Ana.

This place might be pretty hard to leave, actually, if we survived Ricketts's poison.

Caro led us toward the back of the pub, where several small tables were pushed into a line. A group was crowded around one side, leaving seats for the rest of us.

We sat, and Caro introduced us. Names flew too fast for me to keep up with, and people were from all different divisions. While some of the details went in one ear and out the other, it was a good time. The suspicious looks I'd been getting were being replaced with smiles.

After about thirty minutes, I leaned toward Caro. "So, does Cade ever come out?"

"Nah. He's a loner, and too busy fighting in battles and all that."

"Battles?"

"Yeah. God of war. He'll travel the world, fighting on the side he thinks is right."

"Wow."

"Yeah. He made a load of money as an elite mercenary early on, so now he works for the Protectorate and volunteers. For war. He has a nice apartment somewhere around here, but I've never snagged an invite." Her gaze widened on something behind me. "Speak of the devil."

I turned to look. Cade had just stepped inside the bar, his dark hair windswept and his thin sweater molding nicely over his muscles.

I swallowed hard, my mouth suddenly dry.

His head turned toward us. Before we could make eye contact, I whipped my head back around to face my friends. Heat warmed my cheeks, which did *not* fit with my otherwise badass persona.

"Hmmm." Caro's eyebrows wiggled. "I wonder what he's doing here."

Ana's eyes darted between Caro and me. "What? What'd I miss?"

"Well, Cade and Bree spent the day together. Fighting. Bonding while fighting. As one does." Caro grinned widely. "And suddenly here he is! At the bar he never visits, to hang out with people he doesn't like."

"I have no idea what you're talking about," I said.

"Would you get me another drink?" Caro asked.

Before I could answer, I felt my chair get shoved back. I flailed and nearly tipped over, righting myself at the last moment and realizing that Caro had pushed my stool out with her foot.

"Sneaky." But I smiled at her. It was good to have another friend. It made me miss Rowan, but it was good.

Ana and Ali both gave eyebrow waggles. Haris caught sight of them, and though he didn't seem to know what they were waggling about, he joined in, too.

Okay, the good would wear off quick if those three didn't quit it.

I turned and went to the bar, sidling up next to Cade. His stormy scent twined around me, making my eyes flutter. I snapped them open.

Get it together.

This was the perfect opportunity to make it clear—to myself, mostly—that this was just professional. Any wayward hormones I had regarding this guy—this *god*—were to be ignored and avoided. I was going to prove it right now.

Cade looked down at me, his full lips picking up at the side. "I heard you were coming out. What can I get you?"

"Nothing, thanks," I said. "I'm going back in thirty minutes. Need to be up bright and early tomorrow."

"True enough."

"Caro invited us. Said it'd be good to meet some people if we were going to stick around."

"She's right. It's a good group of people."

Deadly people. Their magical signatures had been intense. It really was an elite team.

Sophie came to get his order, and I passed Caro's along as well. She didn't even ask me for my name again—just set up a tab. I hoped the Protectorate would pay for it when I left, then felt a bit guilty immediately. I didn't like to take things that weren't mine. I'd have to sort this out somehow.

While we waited, I looked up at Cade. "So, I heard you don't come here often."

"There was incentive." His voice was slightly rougher than normal.

"Like what?"

"I was thirsty." The slight heat in his gaze suggested that he wasn't thirsty for just whiskey.

Did he mean me?

I shivered, leaning closer to him. Then I pulled back, trying to be subtle about it. Because nope. I wasn't going to touch that one with a ten-foot pole. Relationships had always made me uncomfortable—not to mention the pickings had been slim in Death Valley Junction. And we weren't sticking around anyway.

I especially couldn't get involved with someone as hot and powerful as Cade. It'd be too hard to keep my wits about me.

"Here you go!" Sophie's voice broke the spell that had bound Cade and I together.

I stepped back, cheeks slightly flushed, and turned to her. "Thanks." I grabbed the drinks and looked up at Cade. "Good to see you."

Then I hightailed it out of there.

I delivered the drinks to my friends without looking back once.

"You blew that one," Caro said.

"It went exactly how I wanted it to go." I sipped my Pink Squirrel.

"Hmmm. Well if it were me, I'd have wanted it to end out back in the alley."

Haris and Ali laughed. I choked on my Pink Squirrel.

"What? I know how to go for what I want," Caro said.

"All right, Dirty Spice." Ali patted her on the shoulder.

My jaw dropped. "Was that a Spice Girls joke?"

"What?" Ali asked. "Too dated?"

I held up my hand, thumb and forefinger pinched almost all the way together. "Just a little bit. But you do you."

He saluted, grinning.

Cade had found a seat at another table across the room. Within a few minutes, a dangerous-looking dude joined him. A friend? So maybe he hadn't come here to see me after all.

But every now and again, the side of my neck felt warm. Whenever I glanced over, he wasn't looking at me, but I wasn't convinced that he hadn't *been* looking at me.

We spent the next twenty minutes drinking and chatting, and frankly, I really enjoyed it. Like, a lot.

Whatever happened from here on out, it was nice to have friends like this. A community. Too bad it wouldn't last.

CHAPTER SIX

Caro escorted us back to the Protectorate around eight, leaving everyone else out to party. By the time we stepped out of the portal into the forest, I was truly dead tired. It wasn't even dark yet, and I thought I could sleep for twelve hours.

"Thank you so much," I said.

"No problem." She grinned. "I'll show you to your room."

She led us up to the castle and through the main entry, then up the curved stairs to the second floor.

As we walked, a high-pitched barking sounded.

A second later, three small dogs raced down the stairs on the other side of us. But they were *ghosts*. One had wings. The other devil horns. And the last had really long fangs.

I did a double take. "What are they?"

Caro grinned. "That's Chaos, Ruckus, and Mayhem. Collectively known as the Pugs of Destruction. They've lived here for centuries."

I turned to watch them sprint through the main entry, nails clicking on the floor. "They can cause problems even though they're ghosts?"

"They're professionals."

"All right, then." I continued up the stairs.

She led us down a long hallway into a quiet part of the castle, then into a large room with two double beds. "This is temporary. If you decide to stay, you'll each get your own tower apartment. I've put some spare clothes in the dresser. When you get a chance, you can go shopping for more. I know some good shops in Magic's Bend and Edinburgh."

"Thanks." From here, the bed looked divine.

We said goodnight, and I was in bed within five minutes. I was extremely proud of the fact that I'd found the energy to brush my teeth in the little en suite bathroom.

I stared up at the ceiling. "This is an upgrade, huh?"

"Yeah," Ana said from the bed next to me. "I kinda like it here."

A pale glow lit the room. I sat up and looked at the foot of the bed. A ghost pug stared at me, his face scrunched. His little wings quivered. "Pug of Destruction, huh?"

He wolfed, then farted. I sighed. I loved dogs, hated dog farts. Couldn't have one without the other, even if the dog had been dead for hundreds of years.

I patted the bed near my hip. "You can sleep next to me if you point your butt the other direction."

The dog trundled up and laid down. Then farted again. I smiled, then flopped back on the bed. "Yeah, Ana. I kinda like it here too."

Ghost dog—Mayhem, Chaos, or Ruckus, I wasn't sure which —woofed again.

"I can't believe they chose us," Ana said.

"Me neither." I yawned, hoping I'd be ready to face the day tomorrow. That it'd bring us a cure. "Night, Ana."

"Night, Bree."

The scream tore into my dreams. For a moment, I was back in

Death Valley, tearing across the desert on top of the buggy, fighting off the shrieking bats that lived in the middle of Carter's Canyon. The beasts were ten feet long and howled right before striking with their giant fangs. My sword always got a great workout there.

But then it came again, and this time...

The scream was distinctly human.

My heart leapt into my throat, and my eyes popped open. Darkness.

I flew out of bed, stumbling briefly over my borrowed clothes. "Ana! Are you okay?"

"I'm fine!" She leapt out of bed. "What's that?"

"No idea."

The light of the ghostly pug lit the room. He stood by the door, quivering, then darted through. I raced after him, into the hall. The stone was probably cold on my bare feet, but I didn't notice as I raced down the hall, Ana at my side.

The pug led the way, a weird little warrior who growled deep in his throat. Somehow, it should have been silly. But terror and the dog's seriousness quashed any humor.

As we ran, I drew my sword from the ether and Ana drew her throwing daggers. Though we each had an arsenal stashed in the ether, these were our preferred weapons.

Dim light glowed from the sconces on the wall, but we saw nothing unusual. Just golden light on the stone hallway.

My heart thundered as we rounded the corner. I could *feel* some kind of dark magic on the air—something that was vaguely familiar but also not right. Not for the Protectorate.

A dark streak on the wall caught my eye.

Blood.

And the ground beneath my feet was wet. My stomach dropped. I glanced down.

Water. It gleamed clear.

Thank fates.

Then fear replaced relief.

"*No.*" Only one person that I'd met here fought with water. Caro.

I ran faster, soon catching sight of a figure collapsed on the ground. Platinum hair gleamed in the light of the sconces.

"Caro!" My heart thudded. I skidded to a halt at her side, falling to my knees.

Ana dropped down next to me, panting.

Caro was lying on her front, arms splayed. I swallowed hard, trying to keep my fear from making my hands shake, and carefully turned her over. Ana protected her head from the stone floor. Caro's eyes were closed and her jaw slack.

Blood smeared her forehead from a wound, and a slice across her chest soaked her clothes with blood. My breath heaved, ice racing through me.

Oh, shit!

I tore off my shirt, not even caring that it left me in a tiny camisole. Magic hid the four-pointed star mark at the top of my spine, so I didn't have to worry about anyone seeing it. I pressed my shirt to the wound on her chest.

"Caro! Caro, can you hear me?" I demanded.

Her eyes fluttered open, gleaming silver. Confusion glinted in them, then they cleared. "You."

"Me?"

"Run." Fear glinted in her eyes.

"*No.*" I wouldn't leave her!

"I surprised him." She winced.

"Who?"

She sucked in a ragged breath, her cheeks so pale that she looked ghostly.

"Ana, hold the shirt. I'm going to go get help." I surged to my feet.

Thundering footsteps sounded from behind. I turned. People

poured into the hallway, pushing me aside. They crowded around Caro, kneeling to help.

I stepped back, flattening myself against the wall. Ana joined me.

We looked on, silent and worried. Not part of the group. Which was fair. We were new. But Caro…

I liked her so much.

Fates, would she be okay? And who had done this?

~

As soon as they took Caro away to the infirmary, I found another shirt and immediately started looking for clues. Others were on the job as well—Ali and Haris among them—but I couldn't just do nothing.

The attack had happened at five in the morning, meaning it was already light. The sleep I'd gotten gave me renewed energy, and I used it to scour the grounds, looking for whomever had broken in and hurt Caro. Unfortunately, the blood streaks had petered out and given us no clues, and there was no sign of the attacker themselves.

"There's no way they could have found us," Haris said as we stood outside in the cold, near the forest. "We're blocked by a spell that keeps us entirely invisible to those who would seek the Protectorate."

"So how the hell did they get in?" Ali asked.

"No idea." Haris scrubbed his face, looking weary and sad. "In and out like a ghost. No trace."

I paced, my mind racing. The sun now shone, but the day would feel cold until I knew that Caro was better. This felt bad. Like somehow, it was connected to me.

When a bell sounded from the top of the castle's highest tower, I spun around.

"That's our cue," Ali said. "Meeting time."

We hurried back. My heart thundered as we entered the entry hall. Dozens of people were crowded around, dressed in a variety of clothes ranging from club wear to nightgowns.

Many of them turned suspicious gazes on me and Ana.

New girls.

Ana grabbed my hand and squeezed.

Cade descended the main stairs, his gaze worried, then gestured us forward. "Bree and Ana, come. The meeting is about to begin."

Oh, shit. But I nodded, stepping forward. I wanted answers, and maybe they needed our testimony after finding her.

The crowd parted to let us pass. I felt every stare. I raced to catch up with Cade on the stairs. "How is Caro?"

"Not well."

But not dead. I'd take it. "She'll recover?"

"Aye. She's tough."

Cade led us down a winding hallway toward a large circular room. There was a huge round table and six people within, but my gaze went straight to Caro, who sat in a large chair with a blanket wrapped around her. She was still pale and weak-looking, but her head wound was bound and I couldn't see her chest wound under her shirt. At least the cloth wasn't bloody.

Immediately, I went to her, ignoring the others in the room. "Are you all right?"

"Fine," she croaked. "Had worse than this a dozen times."

"She insisted on coming," Hedy said. "She should be in bed."

"Can't keep me down," Caro said.

A small smile tugged at my lips, and I turned to inspect the room. Besides Cade and Caro, the five leaders of the divisions were here.

I joined them at the table, sitting next to Ana. Worry spread through my chest like tar.

"Do you feel well enough to tell us what happened?" asked

Jude, the one with the star eyes who led the Paranormal Investigative Team.

I gripped the armrest of my chair and looked at Caro.

She sucked in a ragged breath and began. "I wasn't the one he wanted. I shouldn't have even been on that side of the castle, but I couldn't sleep."

"And you ran into a man there?" Jude asked.

"Yes. He was going toward Bree and Ana's room. They're the only ones in that wing. I just ran into him, coming around the corner. He slammed me into the wall and got me with his dagger by the time I realized he wasn't from the Protectorate." She shook her head. "That guy was *fast*. But before he could finish me, I got off one shot. Hit him right in the middle."

"It was enough," Cade said. "He ran for it. There was no trace of him, other than blood and the transportation charm that he dropped."

"Transportation charm?" I asked.

"Yes. Marked with Ricketts's signature mark."

Oh no. Ricketts.

Horrified, I turned wide eyes toward Ana, then the rest of the group. "He was after us." Guilt stabbed me. "I'm so sorry."

Caro shook her head. "Don't be."

"How did he get in?" Ana asked.

"Stanley said the man found him while he was outside the walls, tracking moonflowers," Jude said.

Stanley. The man with the flyaway hair that we'd seen earlier today. The absentminded one.

"He enchanted Stanley and forced him to help him through the gate," Jude continued. "We found Stanley near the wall, the enchantment still on him. He remembered nothing but what the man had made him do."

"But that doesn't explain how the intruder initially found the castle." Cade's voice was different than I'd ever heard it. Harsh, businesslike. "This place is hidden. He shouldn't have even made it to this mountain."

"They found us because Bree and Ana are imbued with the most powerful tracking charms I've ever seen. They defeated even our concealment charms." Hedy's gaze was steady on ours, as if she were watching us to see if we knew anything about this. Jude was giving us the eagle eye as well.

Since my heart and mind had just dropped to the floor in shock and horror, I think I passed her test.

"How?" I whispered. "How is that even possible?"

Ana gripped my hand.

"When Ricketts put the concealment charm on you, did he use your blood?" Hedy asked.

I nodded, remembering the procedure like it was yesterday. Charms could be placed several ways, just like curses. Some were imbued in objects or delivered in a liquid, but particularly strong ones were placed upon the person themselves by using their blood. Only a Blood Sorcerer could do it, and the process was pretty danged creepy.

Hedy nodded. "As I thought. It took a while to run the tests on the sample of strange magic that I found on you yesterday. After the attack, I checked the test and found that Ricketts added a parasite charm—one that piggybacked on the concealment charm that you actually paid for. The tracking charm."

My stomach lurched. "*Oh no.*"

Ana clutched her head. "It ensured he'd always get his payment out of us."

"The intruder managed to find this place because they were looking for *us.* This place was just the bonus." Wow. I felt like *shit.*

"Well done." Jude nodded. "On your deductions, at least. Not on leading a predator here."

I swallowed hard, my throat suddenly tight.

I'd led a predator here. Me. I had done that to Caro. I had to fix it.

"It's odd that they're going to such lengths to find you over a debt," Jude said. "Whoever broke in meant to use that transportation charm to abduct you, we think."

She was right. Ricketts was throwing *everything* at us. Attacks, Lithica poison, kidnappers who could snatch us out of the air.

"Do you have any idea why?" Cade asked.

"It's a lot of money." *Lie.* Though it was, in fact, a lot of money, this had to be something else. This type of enthusiasm on his part indicated a remarkable shift. Did he know what we were?

How could he?

Even we didn't really know. Just that we were something weird and powerful and that changes were coming.

"Cade and I think he's in Venice," I said. "I'm going after them."

"We'll leave soon," Cade said.

"I'm coming," Ana said.

Jude nodded at Cade and me, then leaned forward toward Ana. "Actually, we have a plan that you could help with. You have the charm on you, as well. So we'll set you up in a safe house with guards. If they come for you again, we'll catch them. We need to spread this net as far as we can."

"She's bait?" I almost shrieked the words.

Ana gripped my arm. "Chill, dude. I'll be fine." She nodded, clearly starting to like the plan. "It's actually a good idea. We need to find him—fast. Or we're dead too. If this means we can catch a goon and find out where Ricketts is, it's worth it. You know I can handle this."

I scowled at her. She scowled back. Then I sighed and nodded. If she let me do dangerous shit without too much nagging, I owed her the same.

Family.

And she was right. If this lead didn't pan out, we'd need her.

I looked at Jude. "There will be guards on Ana? Lots of guards?"

"Over two dozen," Jude said. "We'll pull out all the stops. This is our chance to get him. And you're on our team now. We've got your back."

I nodded, both liking this and hating it.

Cade met my gaze. "We're going to have to kill Ricketts when we find him. As long as he lives, the tracking charm will be active on you. Which means you can't return here unless he is dead."

I nodded.

I was an unwitting mole. A time bomb inside the place that had offered me a job and what might be a decent life. Just because I wasn't sure if I wanted that life didn't mean I wanted to hurt this place. Especially considering that the world needed the Undercover Protectorate.

CHAPTER SEVEN

After the meeting, I said goodbye to Ana. "Be safe, okay? We'll catch him, and this will all be over."

"Same. Watch out for yourself. And I love you, nerd."

"Back at you, double-nerd." I turned to Cade. "Ready?"

"Yes. We'll stop at the armory to get that charm, then we're off."

I followed him toward the main stairs, down into the main hall, and then down another wide hall that was paneled with purple silk above dark wood wainscoting.

Magic hit me hard in the chest as we walked, an amazing signature that felt like joy and strength all rolled into one. It was so powerful that it almost made me feel like I was floating.

"What is that?" I asked.

"Um…" He searched for an answer. "You'll find out eventually. It's not my place."

"Does this place have a lot of secrets?"

"Yes. Not many bad ones, though." He led me through a heavy door and down wide stairs into the basement.

"You aren't locking me up, are you?" I hesitated on the stairs.

Was this actually punishment for unwittingly bringing the attacker here?

Cade stopped abruptly and turned, still towering over me despite the fact that he was on the lower stair. His gaze was intense. "No, Bree. I promise. We will not turn on you here. If you don't make the grade, you won't be able to stay. If you do something terrible, there could be disciplinary action. But there'd be a trial. We won't just throw you in the dungeon without warning. We're not the Order of the Magica."

My shoulders relaxed. I didn't like the part about disciplinary action, but the rest made me feel better. "All right. Let's get moving."

He nodded, then turned, leading me down to a wide stone hallway lit by golden torches. A massive wooden door with iron lattice on the front swelled with magic at his touch and spun open.

The large room was full of weapons of every variety—both steel and magical. There were so many, and they were so fabulous, that I almost didn't notice the man working in the corner, bent over a little table with a lamp glowing at the end.

His head popped up, pale eyes gleaming. "Cade! It is almost done."

"Thank you, Coriandar."

"You must be Bree." Coriandar smiled at me. "This amulet should help you control your magic. But its power is not infinite, so you will have to learn to control it yourself, eventually."

"Thank you." I hated that *both* of these men now knew about my issues, but I stepped forward to take the amulet, unwilling to look a gift horse in the mouth.

"Wear it well," Coriandar said. "And it will serve you well."

I wasn't sure what that meant, exactly, but he smiled when I slipped the necklace over my head, so I figured I was doing it all right. "Thank you."

As Cade led me out of the room, my gaze lingered on the

weapons. I loved the katana that had been a gift from my mother, and all my other weapons had been specially chosen. But a girl could dream. One could never have too many weapons.

As we climbed the stairs, Cade murmured, "Coriandar will not share your control issues with anyone else, but you must learn to manage your magic. You were chosen to join the Protectorate because of your determination and fighting ability, and the sheer wealth of magic that you house within you, but you must train hard to wield it well."

I hated hearing it—knowing that I was so flawed—but he was right. My magic was on the fritz, and I had to get it under control. "I know. I will."

When we reached the hall at the top of the stairs, I turned toward Cade. "Ready, now?"

"Aye. I'll lead." He reached for my hand.

I took it, gripping his much larger palm in my own. Heat zinged up my arm, and I averted my gaze, unwilling to make eye contact while dirty thoughts were racing through my head.

Cade threw the charm on the ground, and a sparkling gray smoke rose up. He stepped inside and I followed, gasping as the ether sucked me in and flung me across space.

When I stepped out, we were in a huge, bustling square that was full of people in fabulous costumes. Three massive, ornate buildings surrounded us, with a large body of water making up the fourth side of the square. A tall, beautiful bell tower tolled the hour—four o'clock.

All around me, people jostled. Most were wearing fantastic masks to complete their jewel-toned costumes, and many were lining up in formation. For a parade?

"St. Mark's Square," Cade said. "The central point of the city."

"Busy." What a time of year to choose.

"Aye. And the best place to get a boat. Come on." He gripped my hand tighter and pulled me through the crowd.

We wound through bodies as feathers from headdresses

poked me in the face and glitter landed on my clothes. These Venetians sure knew how to party.

We neared the water, which was actually an extremely large bay from what I could tell, and found rows of boats lined up. We passed the traditional gondolas with their curved ends and headed straight for a cluster of sleek wooden speedboats.

"What, no gondolas?" I asked.

"Those are for stealth. We need speed."

We jumped off the stone quay onto the floating wooden docks. An older man approached, his gray mustache fluttering in the breeze. He was even wearing the striped shirt of a gondolier. "Cade! Long time!"

"Mario!" Cade reached out and shook the man's hand. "We need your fast boat."

"For you, anything." The man made the money motion by rubbing his fingers together. "Because I know you will pay."

"Always." Cade smiled.

"With damage deposit."

"Of course."

Mario gestured to a long, sleek boat built of gleaming wood. The cockpit was open, and it looked like the type of thing an old celebrity would ride around in. "Four hundred horsepower. Just what you're looking for."

"Perfect." Cade pulled a roll of cash out of his pocket and handed some of it over.

My jaw dropped. I was used to seeing big wads of cash—we regularly charged 10k for a ride across Death Valley—and the roll he was carrying was a big chunk of change.

Cade hopped down into the boat and I followed, my gaze sticking to the roll of money.

"You always carry that much with you?" I whispered.

"On jobs like this, aye."

"All right, then." I found a spot next to the steering wheel and held on to the metal rail. There wasn't much space in the boat—

most of that was taken up by the engine compartment. Cade waved goodbye to Mario, who threw off the lines. He pulled us away from the dock, then we joined the rest of the boats in the harbor.

It was slow going at first, weaving between the party boats that were full of dancing revelers.

"Where are we going?" I shouted over the wind.

"Poveglia Plague Island."

"Plague Island?!"

"No longer. But it was once used as a quarantine. They say that half the soil is made of decomposing bodies."

"Ugh." I shuddered. All those poor people.

"Now, it's the home of the Vampire of Venice." We reached an open area in the bay, and he pulled on the throttle. The engine roared and the boat punched ahead, flying over the water like a race car.

The wind whipping my hair back from my face was so loud that it was impossible to talk. But whoever the Vampire of Venice was, I probably wasn't going to like him. Vampires were a rarely seen species, since they often hung out in their own realm. I'd only ever met one in real life.

We raced across the sea, heading toward a small island that was pretty far out. I kept glancing at Cade, who looked natural out here on the open water, with his dark hair whipping in the breeze and his gaze focused on the water ahead.

As we neared the island, which was quite small, I made out the building that sat on the only hill. It looked old, eighteenth or nineteenth century, and there was a depressing air about the place.

Cade slowed the boat and pulled toward a large dock that jutted out into the water.

A figure came striding down the dock as we neared, hooves thudding against the wooden slats. His top half looked like that of a bull.

"Holy fates, is that a Minotaur?" I asked.

"Only one there is," Cade said.

"So, *the* Minotaur. The one from Greek myth?"

"Aye. And now gainfully employed."

"All right, then."

"Who goes there?" the Minotaur roared. His voice was rough and loud, carrying with it a serious threat. I'd fought way bigger monsters than him, but still, I shifted nervously.

"Bree Blackwood and Cade," Cade shouted.

"Oh!" The Minotaur bowed low. "Welcome, god of war."

"Thank you." Cade pulled the boat up alongside the dock and tossed the rope to the Minotaur.

The air of threat surrounding the beast had lifted, no doubt because he respected the hell out of Cade. But he didn't respect me yet, so I kept an eye on him as I climbed onto the dock.

Cade followed. "We're here to see the Vampire of Venice."

"Of course." The Minotaur gestured to indicate the dock that led to the island.

We set off toward land, which looked like a wild, abandoned island. The building on top of the hill looked even more haunted and decrepit from here. Torches blazed at the entrance, a spooky invite to a party to which I'd rather RSVP 'no.'

"The Vampire of Venice has eccentric tastes," I said, poking around for some details.

"This was once an insane asylum," the Minotaur said. "Back in the nineteenth century."

"Oh, bummer." I frowned. "Sad."

"Sad?" Cade asked. "Most people would say creepy or cool."

"Well, asylums were never great places, were they? Most of the people just had epilepsy or other conditions that weren't a threat to anyone. They just needed treatment. But they got locked up here instead." I shivered, sadness for those poor souls filling me.

"You're very empathetic," Cade said.

"I don't know. It's just sad, okay?" I searched for a way to get the subject off me.

"Empathy," Cade said.

I punched him lightly on the shoulder, surprisingly comfortable with him.

As we neared the house, I swore I could feel the ghosts that haunted it. I shuddered, *really* not wanting to go inside.

I quickened my pace. Best to get it over with.

The Minotaur led us up the expansive steps to the massive front doors, which creaked open to admit us.

"Like a freaking haunted house," I muttered.

I stepped into a fabulous entryway. The huge, glittering chandelier alone had to be worth every penny I'd ever earned in my whole life. Shining marble floors gleamed, and priceless paintings decorated the walls.

"Some asylum," I muttered.

"The Vampire of Venice has made some modifications in the years since her great ancestor lived on this island," the Minotaur said. "The original Vampire of Venice. Fiametta de Bastian, died in 1576. Her ancestors now form one of the most powerful families in the Venetian underworld."

"And we're going to meet the boss?" I murmured to Cade.

"Aye."

The Minotaur led us to the back of the house, into a huge office decorated in navy and gold. A woman sat behind the desk. She rose when we entered.

She was slim as a skeleton, with pale skin stretched tight over prominent cheekbones. She wore a sleek black suit that buttoned up to her neck, with her ebony hair slicked back in a long ponytail. Of course her skin was pale and her lips blood red. White fangs barely showed. All in all, she made a fabulous picture of a vampire mob boss.

"Cade." Her voice dripped with ice, but it was somehow warm.

Even when she was being welcoming, she sounded like a stone-cold bitch.

I liked her. This woman got shit done.

Her gaze moved to the Minotaur. "You may go, Mino."

The beast bowed and left.

"Vittoria de Bastian." Cade bowed. "It is good to see you again."

"And you," she purred icily. I didn't know how she managed to make a purr icy, but I did know that I didn't like that purr.

Dang it. I'd have kicked myself if I could. No reason to feel jealousy over Cade. That was stupid. And dangerous.

"And who are you?" Vittoria turned her blazing blue eyes on me.

"I am Bree Blackwood. And we're here because we need your help."

"Hmmm. Straight to the point." She gestured us toward her desk. "I like it."

I strolled toward her, Cade at my side. She watched me coolly, properly interpreting the threat that I posed. A lot of people underestimated me—which I liked—but not Vittoria.

I respected that.

She sank elegantly into her chair. It was a massive affair of carved wood that matched her hulking desk. Both were so ornate that they made my eyes bleed, but it was the colorful glass lamps that took the cake for gaudy. It wasn't my taste, but I had to say that it suited the Vampire of Venice.

Cade and I sat in the large red chairs in front of her desk.

"What can I do for you?" she purred.

"We're looking for Ricketts," Cade said. "We've heard that his base is here in Venice. Since you know everything about the underworld in your city, we're hoping you can tell us where he is."

"Ricketts." She sneered. "That interloper."

"Interloper?" I asked.

"Yes." She spat the word. "My family and the other great families of Venice—the Zanotta, the Contarini, and the Badoera—have been running the supernatural crime world here for *centuries*. Then that newcomer arrived..." The disgust in her voice would be worthy of an Oscar. I could *feel* the loathing. "He breaks the laws of our kind. Targets the weak and the poor."

"You don't do that?"

"No!" She scowled. "The weak and the poor have no money. And there's honor in what we do. There are plenty of evil bastards to wring for all they're worth."

A mob boss with a conscience. I'd like her if she weren't occasionally shooting Cade hot looks.

"In addition to stepping on our business, Ricketts has found a way to wring pennies from the poor and to prey on the most vulnerable." Her red lips twisted.

"Why don't you stop him?" I asked.

She scoffed. "Do I look like Wonder Woman to you? I am a businesswoman. Not a charity."

"Wouldn't you want to kill him if he's cutting into your bottom line?" I knew I was giving her twenty questions, but I really wanted to know what this woman's deal was.

"Of course I'd love to take him out. I even know where he lives—it took me ages to find that. But he's as powerful as I am now, because of his magic. As powerful as all the families. That makes him our equal, and it allows him to enter the pact." Her gaze sharpened. "We will not engage in assassination attempts against other families. Else how can we ever be safe ourselves?"

"Hmmm. Smart." I nodded.

"Vittoria has always been clever," Cade said.

"What do you want with Ricketts?" she said.

"To kill him." I grinned.

Her eyes brightened with interest, and I swore she almost clapped. "Really? Perfect. You're outsiders with motivation who cannot be traced back to me. The perfect ones to do the job."

"Does that mean you'll tell us where he is?" I asked.

"Of course. In exchange for something," she said.

"We're killing your enemy." I made my voice hard. "That's enough."

Her gaze drifted to Cade, turning sultry. "Perhaps just a small token of your appreciation for my assistance, then." She leaned across the desk toward Cade, whispered in his ear.

I resisted the desire to smack her away—really, jealousy did not become me—and stewed in my seat.

She sank back behind her desk.

Cade gave her an impassive gaze. "I'll consider it."

She nodded, clearly content. "You can find Ricketts at San Zaccaria."

I frowned. "A church?"

"*Under* the church." She shook her head. "The idiot has built his headquarters under the church."

"Wouldn't that flood?" I asked. "Venice is on the water."

"Exactly. It is moronic. He uses magic to shore up his defenses, but one day they will fail. It is unnatural to be underground in Venice!"

She was clearly *very* bothered by this. I couldn't blame her.

"Any other details that you can share?" Cade asked.

"Yes. You should enter via the Grand Canal and the back canals. It is a windier route through the city, but the other way is blocked by poltergeists. From our reconnaissance, I've learned that there are two statues at the entrance of the church. They are guards, not decoration, meant to scare away supernaturals. Incapacitate them, then find the church's basement. From there you must make your way past enchanted blockades. But I know no more."

"Thank you." Cade stood.

I followed.

Vittoria eyed Cade, her gaze burning. "Remember that I want that date."

He nodded, but said nothing, and we hurried from the room. I could feel Vittoria's gaze on our backs. At least she hadn't eyed our necks while we'd been in there.

When we reached the outside, I sucked in the fresh air gratefully. It was hot and humid, but at least it wasn't the heavy perfume that cloaked the old asylum.

The Minotaur led us to the boat, and we sped back across the bay as the sun set, cutting across water that glowed as orange as the sky. Venice loomed on the horizon, fabulously beautiful.

I'd never been to a place like this—never made it off the West Coast, in fact—but it was fantastic.

Near the city, Cade piloted us between the other boats full of revelers, entering the Grand Canal. It was massive, surrounded on both sides by huge mansions. The canal itself was crowded with boats, all decked out for the parade.

"At least this will allow us to slip through undetected," Cade said. "With so many people here, we'll blend."

I nodded, taking in everything, keeping a wary gaze out for threats.

There were supernaturals and humans here, all mixing as one, though the humans had no idea. The costumes made it possible for the supernaturals to come out in droves, many wearing their natural wings and horns. It was risky, but I couldn't blame them.

Cade pulled his phone out of his pocket and typed something in.

"Calling someone?" I asked.

"Google maps. I have no idea where this church is."

"Smart."

A few moments later, Cade turned our boat onto one of the smaller canals, edging past gondolas with inches to spare. At least this boat was very narrow.

We motored slowly under an ornate bridge that was covered by a roof. On top, four men fought a vicious fistfight, while onlookers cheered.

"Tradition," Cade said. "Going back to the Middle Ages."

One of the fighters took a hit so hard that he flew off the bridge, splashing into the water below us.

"Aaaand that's the goal of the whole thing," Cade said.

"Not bad."

"Not at all." Cade directed the boat through increasingly smaller canals, taking us deeper into the city. Soon, the streets were empty and the golden lamps positioned farther and farther apart. The sound of revelry disappeared. Beautiful buildings crowded either side of the canals, and balconies hung with laundry that fluttered in the breeze.

We motored under a bridge. As we came out the other side, a thud sounded behind us.

I spun, catching sight of a gray-skinned demon wearing a black leather jumpsuit. His horns were sawed off, and his hand glowed with strange green light. Since his magic already felt like a headache, it'd probably knock me straight out if he hit me with it.

"Ricketts wants you," he hissed, foul breath wafting toward me.

"Duh." But I'd be going to him on my terms.

As he raised his hand, I called upon my magic, grateful for the charm Cade had given me. It allowed me to grasp my magic quickly and fire a tiny burst that knocked him off his feet.

Wow! Like old times.

He slammed onto the stern of the boat, and I lunged to grab him before he could fall into the canal.

I dragged him toward me by the arm, calling my dagger from the ether, and pressed it to his neck.

He was still gasping from the shock of my sonic boom. It felt roughly like your insides were being pulverized, from what people had told me.

"Where is Ricketts's headquarters?" I poked the tip of the

dagger into his neck. I trusted the Vampire of Venice, but it didn't hurt to double-check. Not when the stakes were so high.

"Never telling you," he hissed.

"Sure you will." I lowered the dagger to his crotch. "I'll castrate you before I send you back to hell."

Actually, the idea made vomit rise in my throat. But this always worked on dudes.

His yellow eyes flared bright. "San Zaccaria!"

I grinned, then stabbed him in the throat and shoved him overboard.

Pain suddenly gouged me in the chest, spreading outward like knives, and I gripped the boat. My heart felt like it stopped beating. Tears filled my eyes as I sucked in a shallow breath.

But it wouldn't go in.

I couldn't breathe!

The Lithica poisoning was really hitting me now. Panic flared in my mind.

Then the pain stopped.

I sucked in a ragged breath, finally able to get air into my lungs.

Holy fates, that'd been scary. It'd only been a few seconds, but it'd been so visceral.

Turning to stone would be a nightmare. No wonder people eventually caved and went to Ricketts for the cure.

I stood shakily and dusted off my hands, then stored my dagger in the ether and pulled the pain potion from my pocket. I swallowed the whole thing in one gulp, blessed relief finally flowing through me. At least temporarily.

I went to stand next to Cade.

"Good work," Cade said, clearly having not noticed me. He'd been in front of me. "By the time he wakes up in hell, it'll be too late to warn Ricketts that we're coming."

"I guess he's still sending goons after us." Why was he

suddenly so interested in us? I worried at my lip. "You're sure they've got a lot of guards on Ana?"

"More than two dozen. And they'll put her somewhere secure." He glanced at me, understanding in his eyes. "I'm sorry that you're worried."

"She's tough. Stronger than me, actually. I shouldn't worry."

"You did well with the charm."

"Thanks for getting it." It might be a temporary fix, but it was amazing to be in control again. No way in hell I'd use it underground—I didn't trust it that much—but it was nice to have up here.

We really needed to succeed, and I'd take whatever weapon I could get.

Cade pulled the boat over to a small floating dock. "We'll go on foot from here. Too narrow after this point."

I got out of the boat and climbed the five stone steps up to the main sidewalk. There were no cars in Venice, not that any would fit on this little walkway.

Cade climbed out and tied the boat off, then joined me. We set off down the walkway, going deeper into the city. Cade took one more look at his phone, then tucked it into his pocket. "We're nearly there."

We turned right into an alley, the buildings looming on either side. Eventually, it spilled out into a large square, with a huge church across the way. The place was entirely empty save for two guards.

They looked like stone statues, but when I reached out for the signature of their magic, I caught the slightest whiff of rotting garbage.

"Ew," I whispered.

"Evil," Cade murmured.

Yep. The darkest magic always smelled like a dumpster fire.

I reached for Cade's hand, pulling him close to me and

leaning in, swaying. "Pretend we're drunk. Just some lost tourists."

"Smart."

Maybe. They were only supposed to repel supernaturals, and this might not trick them. But at least we could try. And I didn't hate being pressed up against Cade, even as I knew it was a bad idea.

I'd been alone a long time and Cade was...well, Cade.

We ambled closer to the statues. Cade's heat singed me, but I did my best to ignore it, focusing instead on the statues.

"Holy fates," I whispered. "They're not alive."

"No."

The guards were meant to look like statues—and they did—but something about their magical signature was distinctly dead. Maybe it was the scent of rot?

It was subtle, whatever it was. If Cade and I hadn't had such strong magic ourselves, we wouldn't have been able to sense it.

"Go for the kill, then," I said. Because whatever magic had been used to reanimate these corpse guards, it was some dark stuff.

"Agreed."

We stumbled up the steps, keeping our charade going till the last moment. When our feet landed on the top step, dim light swirled around the guards. The stone veneer covering them chipped away, and their magic surged forth. Their bodies were half decayed, with maggots crawling out of their empty eye sockets.

I gagged at the stench, fear racing through me, chilling my skin. I used it as my cue, breaking away from Cade and calling on my sonic boom power.

I hurled a defined blast at the nearest zombie-thing, letting Cade take care of the other.

It slammed the guard into the wall behind, but he just pulled himself off and grinned at me.

Damn it. Couldn't pulverize the insides of the undead, it seemed. If I wanted to really blow him apart, I'd also have to take out the historic church.

Not an option.

I drew my daggers from the ether. Given the choice, I wouldn't get anywhere near a zombie.

I threw the blade, which sank into its neck, but the creature kept coming. Fast.

Right. Too good to be true. Dismemberment was the way to go.

I stashed my second dagger in the ether and drew my sword, swinging for the zombie's head. My blade sailed through the decayed sinew and flesh, cutting through bone. The head tumbled to the ground with a thud, but there was no arterial blood spray.

Hey, that was convenient.

I could get down with killing zombies.

But the thing kept coming, almost upon me. The stench was gag-worthy.

My heart pounded as I danced back and slashed for the legs, taking out the left one. My blade couldn't cut entirely through the right leg, and the creature reached for me. It gripped my non-sword arm. Pain flared.

"Ow!"

The thing had an iron grip. It squeezed until stars flashed in my eyes and I thought my bones might break.

Awkwardly, I swung my blade at the arm that gripped me, severing the limb at the elbow. Then I kicked the creature in the chest, sending him crashing backward onto the stone portico.

The beast began to crawl toward me on its last remaining leg and arm.

"Oh, hell no." I leapt toward it, severing the arms and then the leg.

Finally, it lay still.

I stood, panting. The severed arm still clutched my bicep. It'd stopped squeezing, but its grip was so strong that my eyes watered. I tried yanking at it, but it held tight. Then I tried prying the fingers off. No dice.

Freakin' zombie strength.

Panting, I turned toward Cade.

His zombie was in about twenty pieces, and definitely not moving anymore. In fact, it was already starting to disappear. Magic, I had to guess. Didn't want the humans finding zombie bits. That was the trouble with living in a mixed community—hiding the magic was difficult. The Order didn't allow that kind of negative press with humans, though, so it was necessary.

"Nicely done." I pointed at the disgusting arm hanging off my own. "But could I get a little help here?"

Cade winced at the sight of the zombie arm gripping my bicep.

"Yeah." I grimaced. "It stinks like a two-month old tuna salad had a baby with a diaper."

"Descriptive." Cade approached and quickly pried the fingers away from my arm. He tossed the limb away.

I sagged. "Thanks."

"No problem."

He wiped his sword on one of the fallen zombie's ragged shirt, getting rid of the gore. I retrieved the dagger I'd thrown and wiped it off, too.

Technically, I didn't have to retrieve it—the expensive magic that kept it stored in the ether would collect it for me. But next time I used it, it'd be covered in whatever blood or gore it had collected the last time. Adding a cleaning spell had been too expensive.

Cade turned to the massive wooden doors of the church and pulled one open, slipping inside.

I followed, immediately enveloped in the cool darkness. The

scent of candles and wood polish surrounded me. In the distance, lights glowed on the stained glass. The air was so still and silent.

"There's no one here," I whispered.

"There will be more challenges below."

"He's good with his spells." Ricketts's magic had proven that he was a badass. I wasn't looking forward to whatever waited for us.

I crept around to the side of the church, looking for stairs that would lead down. A nondescript door caught my eye, but when I tugged on the door handle, it didn't open.

"Locked." I ran my fingers around the door seam, feeling a prickle of magic. "By a spell."

Cade approached, spreading his hand out over the door. I stepped aside as he closed his eyes and his magic swelled. The scent of a storm at sea washed over me. He stepped back. "It's protected by an incantation. We need to know the words to unlock the door."

"Hmmm. We're not going to figure that out."

"It's not a problem." He pressed both palms to the door, and his magic flared around him.

This was different, though. Darker.

His eyes blazed black, their usual green hue drowned out by darkness. I stumbled backward as his magic brushed my skin, filling my mind with visions of battle and blood and death.

Magic burst on the air, the spell that protected the door breaking.

I leaned against the wall, letting the horrible images of death and war fade from my mind. Cade turned to me.

"Whoa." I panted, still shocked by the way his magic had changed. The darkness of it. "You broke through that spell."

"God of war." His face was serious. "In a sense, that means god of death. Nothing like the true gods of death, but I can use that power to kill some spells. Not complex ones, but that one wasn't complex."

"Wow. That's actually kind of scary."

"I know." He smiled grimly. "Useful, though." He tried the door, but it was locked by a plain old human lock. So he stepped back, as if he were going to charge the door.

I grabbed his shoulder. "Hang on. I've got it."

He stepped back, and I approached the door, digging into my pocket for my wallet. I pulled out two narrow picks, then stuck them in the lock.

It took a few seconds, but I finally found the pin.

I pressed.

It clicked.

The lock disengaged.

I twisted the door open and grinned, then stuck the picks back in my wallet.

"Well done," he said. "How'd you learn that?"

"I'm not a cat burglar, if that's what you're wondering."

He raised his hands. "Hey, I know you're on the right side of the law."

"Hmmm." I scrunched up my face into a doubtful expression. "Sort of."

"Exactly. I just aid and abet the criminals in their escape to Hiders Haven." I shrugged. "And anyway, I don't always agree with the Order of the Magica." They'd once hunted my friend Cass, and she was a decent person. "So if folks are running from them, I'll help."

"Fair enough. I'm not on their side. So you learned that as a hobby?"

"In my childhood." For when we needed a place to sleep after our mother had been killed. But I wouldn't be telling him that.

"A story for another time."

"Sure." *Not.* I started down the staircase, ready to end the conversation.

Dim wall sconces lit the way. The air became cooler and damper as we went.

At the bottom was a plain room built of rough stone. My boots splashed into water. I crinkled my nose. It smelled *wet*. And muddy. The air was damper, and I could imagine all the water in Venice, pushing at these walls, held back by magic.

"This is the stupidest thing ever." *Underground in Venice?* Idiot. "Magic can only hold back the water for so long."

"Agreed."

We stood still for a moment, inspecting the room, swords drawn and ready for anything. There were no doors or windows. Just a plain room. Some boxes were piled against the wall, slowly rotting away.

I frowned. "He's tried to make this look like storage."

"There must be a hidden door." Cade sloshed toward one wall, inspecting it.

I trudged over to the other wall, grimacing at the feel of the water around my calves, flowing into my boots. I pressed my hands to the stone wall, feeling for any kind of magic.

I didn't find it until I reached the far wall—the slight pulse of magic that indicated a spell of some kind. "Over here, Cade."

He splashed toward me, then ran his big hand over the wall.

As he studied the magic, I rubbed my foot against the base of the wall under the water, searching for some kind of lever that might ignite the magic to open the door. The water was too murky to see through, but my toe slipped into a crevice in the wall.

"Jackpot." I grinned.

"What is it?"

"I think it's a lever." I pressed my toe into the divot, hitting a little soft spot that depressed slightly under pressure. I could feel magic around it.

"Underwater?" he asked.

"Yeah. Right where my left leg is." I stepped back so he could test it.

He found the divot with his toe. "There's magic around it."

113

His leg flexed slightly—which was pretty easy to see since he had the muscular legs that you'd expect on a god of war or an Olympic wrestler—and magic flared around the door. It glowed a pale white, then the whole thing disappeared.

Wall sconces burst to life, flames flaring brightly on the walls of the room.

"Whoa." I stepped back.

The room within was full of bones.

CHAPTER EIGHT

"It's one of the decorated crypts," Cade said. "Like in Rome."

My gaze traced over the space, which was about the size of the entry hall back at the castle, with columns supporting the arched ceiling.

Every wall and the entire ceiling was covered by thousands of bones, all laid out in decorative patterns. There were swirls made of skulls, geometric shapes made of leg bones, and even some full skeletons dressed like monks. They were pinned to the walls with attachments I couldn't see. Ragged brown robes hung loose around their forms, and their skulls grinned at us. In the ceiling, a headless jeweled skeleton was the centerpiece. Like the room we stood within, the water was about calf level.

"Monks," Cade said.

"This must be why Ricketts built his headquarters here. And the magic keeping this place from flooding is older than we expected. It might not be his at all."

"Aye. Ricketts chose well. There will be an enchantment in there. Something to keep us from passing."

I glanced at Cade, struck again by his strong competence. We were technically underwater and about to walk into the lion's den, facing magic meant to destroy us, and Cade didn't look a bit worried.

Me, on the other hand?

I was shaking in my boots.

Whelp, that's my cue.

"Let's do this thing." I leapt into the room, sword raised in front of me.

Magic exploded in the air. All around, the skeletons burst to life. The robed monks that were attached to the walls jumped down to the floor first, their skeletal hands reaching for us.

I lunged for one, slicing out with my blade. I severed the thing's spine, and it tumbled into the water. Another came from behind it. I took the head, but it kept coming. So I went for the spine again. It collapsed.

"Go for the spine!" I said.

At my side, Cade fought like a tornado, his sword flying and bones clattering.

I hated to see the destruction of something as historic as the crypt, but if this was magic, it'd probably go right back to normal once we were gone.

Sweat dampened my skin as I swung my sword, every strike colliding with a skeleton. Their bones fell into the water, which wasn't as muddy in this room. Beneath the surface, I could see the bones of the skeletons crawling across the ground to knit back together.

As they reformed, more bones broke off the walls and formed more skeletons. They charged us, dozens at a time.

I panted, trying to keep them off of me.

"Back to back!" I shouted.

Cade and I lined up with our backs to each other, fighting off the skeletons that came at us in a circle.

One skeleton wasn't too scary. But masses of them? Some wearing the ragged robes of ancient monks?

Yeah, creepy.

As I sliced through the spine of one skeleton, another got ahold on my arm. Like the zombie, it squeezed with a grip that could crush titanium. My eyes watered as I heaved my sword at the attacking skeleton, slicing down through its arm and straight through its spine.

The thing splashed into the water, but the arm hung on.

This was a trend that I didn't love, but at least it didn't stink like the zombie arm. I wasn't going to look a gift skeleton in the mouth.

Bones clattered all around us as our swords whirled, but the skeletons kept coming. When one grabbed my calf, Cade's huge sword swung down and demolished the creature. A few moments later, I kept one from grabbing his arm.

We weren't a bad team.

Not that it was helping us win.

"There are too many!" I panted. "They keep reforming."

"The magic's too strong."

Bones splashed into the water all around, but the masses of skeletons clawed for us, trying to make it past our whirling blades. They'd overwhelm us soon, drowning us in the shallow water. My heart thundered as sweat dripped down my spine.

There had to be a way to stop these beasts. Something we'd missed. A trigger that would keep the magic in the room from igniting.

Maybe I should have thought of that before leaping in, but I was Pavlov's dog. Instead of drooling at dinner, I leapt into the fight when I felt scared.

Usually, very handy.

Now? Not so much.

I scanned the room as I swung my sword, breaking skeletons on autopilot.

A glint of something shiny caught my eye on the ground near the door. There a bejeweled skull under the water, the sapphires glinting in the low light of the wall sconces.

It was pressed up against the wall, where an unwitting intruder wouldn't be able to see it before stepping in. But if you knew it was there, you could grab it.

I glanced up, to the space where the only jeweled skeleton had been. He was starting to come alive, dragging himself off the wall. But he had no head.

Unlike the other skeletons, he held a massive sword in his hand. The thing gleamed wickedly, its blade as sharp as mine.

Oh, dang.

A skeleton with a blade like that was gonna be trouble.

I glanced at the gleaming skull on the floor, then up at him. An idea flared.

"Cade! There's a skull covered in jewels on the ground by the door. We have to get it and put it on the skeleton that's trying to climb off the ceiling."

Cade hesitated half a second, no doubt checking out the skeleton above and the head by the door. "You go. I'll guard!"

"Okay!"

Cade flew into action, stowing his sword in the ether and grabbing a skeleton by the arms. "Duck!"

I did as he commanded. He swung the skeleton in a circle over my head using it to batter the other skeletons. He spun so fast that it was like a helicopter above me. It collided with our attackers, sending them flying back. They crashed into the walls and splashed into the water. It was like the whole place had exploded.

Whoa.

I shook off my shock and stowed my sword in the ether, then raced for the bejeweled skull, Cade clearing the way. Water splashed high as I sprinted and lunged for the skull.

I grabbed it up, the gems and gold cutting into my hand, and spun back to the middle of the room.

All of the skeletons were in the water. *He'd gotten them all.*

The skeletons were already slowly getting to their feet, but he'd bought us some time.

"Come on!" Cade stood beneath the jeweled skeleton that had almost pulled itself away from the bindings that kept it attached to the ceiling.

I ran for him, the skull clutched tight in my hand. This was like that scene from *Dirty Dancing*, but with more skeletons.

Cade made a platform out of his hands, and I leapt onto it. He heaved me into the air. I stretched, reaching for the skeleton.

I slammed the skull onto his neck, then fell. Cade caught me before I splashed into the water.

The bejeweled skeleton stiffened, then flattened itself against the ceiling and froze. All around us, the bones flew back to the walls, pinning themselves back in place.

I panted, holding on to Cade's neck. I glanced at him.

He grinned at me.

I was filled with this insane desire to kiss him. Just press my lips against his fuller ones and see if was as good as I expected. It probably would be.

Bad idea.

I pushed away from him. "I'm good."

He set me down, his breathing growing steadier. "Quick thinking."

"Thanks. Good job on the skelecopter you had going there."

He chuckled. "Skelecopter?"

"Sometimes I'm clever. But how'd you think of that?"

"Once I realized that they were pretty strong, I figured it was worth a try. Ready to keep going?"

"Yeah." I sloshed toward the exit. "This makes me miss the desert."

"Don't like water?"

"Nope!" It was one reason this place freaked me out so much. "Not water like this! Too used to sand." Though I actually really liked the Highlands. That place was pretty sweet.

I stopped at the entrance to the next room, peering inside. There were fewer sconces in here, just enough to illuminate the place with a gloomy glow. It was a huge vaulted space, nearly as long as a football field. Stone statues sat in nooks against the walls, presiding over sarcophagi.

I inspected the whole space, looking for some kind of lever or way to stop whatever enchanted the massive room.

"I don't see anything from here," Cade said.

"Me neither." If there was a way to stop this room from lighting up, it was impossible to see from our vantage point. "Maybe it's against the wall near this door? Like the last room."

"Maybe." But his voice was doubtful.

So was I. "Let's go in and check near the door. You look left, I'll look right. If there's nothing there, we keep going. Take it as it comes." I hated just waiting here, trying to figure out what would attempt to kill us.

Let's get this over with!

Cade looked at me, his green eyes seeming to see right through me. He nodded. "On three."

I counted down, leaping into the room on *one*. I looked left. "Nothing!"

"Nothing!" Cade said.

We ran, sprinting for the other exit. I gave it my all, hoping to outrun whatever monster would come for us.

But nothing came alive. It was eerily silent except for our splashing footsteps. The dim crypt was creepy, but the threat was invisible.

I slogged through the water, panting and sweating. Gosh, this was getting harder.

Oh, shit.

I glanced down. My heart dropped as my skin chilled with fear. "The water is rising!"

It was up to my knees now. *That's* why the threat was silent.

I pumped my arms and legs, lungs burning as I ran. But it was almost to my middle thighs. And we weren't even halfway across.

Cade was running—the guy had almost a foot on me—but he was holding back. For me.

But the exit was too far. We'd never make it. I could try to swim it, but at this rate….

I'd drown.

But Cade didn't have to.

"Go!" I screamed. "You're faster than me!"

I was barely able to run now. Water was to my thighs. Soon, I'd be wading.

"Go!"

Instead, Cade grabbed me around the waist and threw me onto his shoulder. Then he ran, sprinting across the water like a running back on speed. I hung on, bouncing like mad as water splashed all around.

But the water kept rising. Faster and faster.

I had to shift to keep my head out of the water, inching around so that I could see how far we were from the exit.

Too far.

We weren't going to make it. Not before we had to swim, and unless he was part shark, we wouldn't do that fast enough.

The water was rising, cold and wet. I could feel it all around. It would drown us. It was so close. In my chest, in my mind.

Use it, a voice whispered. *Use it.*

I blinked.

What the heck?

The water is yours.

I shook my head. Was I having a panic attack? I was a scaredy-cat about a lot of things, but I only freaked out *before* the main event. Not during. During the disaster, I was usually cold as ice.

The water is yours.

Holy fates, that was a voice inside my head. And I could feel the water. In my heart, in my head. It was part of me. Like my magic. It filled me, wanting to burst out. Magic, water, magic, water.

I couldn't tell the difference.

And I had no idea what was happening. But something was changing within me. There was more magic in me. Or it was trying to burst out. Or *something.*

I went on instinct, throwing my hands out and forcing the magic from me.

"Go!" I screamed, directing all my magic and fear and rage at the water.

It parted around us, like I was freaking Moses and this was the Red Sea.

Cade stumbled briefly, then adjusted to dry land and sprinted full out like a freight train. I lost my grip on him and flopped back over his shoulder, my head near his lower back. I clung to his waist.

The water held back on either side, a murky brown that threatened to crash in and drown us. But my magic held it at bay, something I didn't understand but sure as hell knew was happening because of me.

I bounced along on his shoulder, feeling like my ribs would break, and forced my magic to keep the water from crashing down on us. It felt like the water was part of me—like I could command it the way I'd command my sonic boom.

But this was easily the least dignified way to learn that I had a new power.

Cade sprinted through the exit, leaping at the last moment and landing on higher ground. Solid, dry ground. I let go of my magic.

In the room behind us, the water crashed down, massive waves colliding together. Fortunately, the water staying in the other room, magic keeping it from flooding the whole place.

Cade set me down on a wood platform. I righted myself, panting and probably red-faced.

Around us, dark water sloshed. We were in a long room. Though it was full of water, there was a large platform built over it, leaving a channel of water on either side.

"What the hell was that?" Cade asked.

"Um." I glanced at him, unsure of how to respond. A noise in the distance caught my attention. I looked around Cade, catching sight of four large figures coming toward us on the large wooden platform. I looked back at Cade. "We've got company."

He turned, drawing his sword from the ether.

"Guards," he muttered.

I drew my daggers, preferring the long-range game. I was getting tired.

In the dim light of the wall sconces, I made out four demons. All an unrecognizable species, but their horns made it pretty clear where they'd come from.

And where they'd be going back to.

While I hesitated to kill other supernaturals, demons were another matter altogether. Because you couldn't kill a demon. All you could do was kill its earthly form. It'd disappear and wake up in its original hell almost immediately. Where they were supposed to be, anyway, since demons weren't allowed to roam the earth. Mainly because they did shit like this—working for evil masterminds. They'd eventually blow our cover with the humans.

So killing a demon was pretty much guilt-free all around. Like low-fat yogurt. Except more murdery. And tastier, because that yogurt sucked. All the smiling women on the commercials could not fool me.

The four demons lumbered toward us, their magic powering up and filling the room with its stench. They were all huge, each a different species. One with red skin, one with blue, and two dark gray ones.

I hurled one of my blades at the nearest demon. It sank into his neck, and he collapsed back, crashing to the wooden platform.

His companions roared and charged us.

Cade answered with his own roar, charging with his blade raised.

Whoa, big fella.

He took out the first demon he met by slicing it right through the middle. I gagged, then raised my dagger.

Before I could get off my shot, a demon threw a fireball toward me. His flame-red skin should have given me a clue.

I dove, skidding against the wooden boardwalk as the fireball sailed overhead. It singed my cheek as it passed. Pain flared briefly.

I scrambled to my feet as he charged up his next fireball, then threw my blade. It sailed through the air, end over end, and landed in his neck.

He gurgled and collapsed backward, thudding onto the wide wooden platform.

Necks were my favorite. Gruesome, but they got the job done. No one kept fighting with a dagger sticking out of their neck.

The last demon—one with pale blue skin—hurled a huge icicle at Cade, but he blocked it with his blade. The thing exploded in the air, raining ice down on Cade as he swiped out with his massive blade.

The demon's blue head flew into the air, blood spraying. It splashed against Cade's face and torso.

Gag. Yup. Zombies were better. No blood.

I trotted toward Cade. "You really like to go for the most gruesome kills, huh?"

"I play to my strengths. And gory casualties seem to be my strength."

I grimaced, though he was right. A guy of his size and muscle power didn't need to get fancy with the footwork.

He stepped closer to me, raising a hand to my burned cheek.

He didn't touch, but I swore I could feel a caress all the same. "Are you all right?"

I swallowed hard and stepped back. "Fine."

He gave me a long look, then knelt at the edge of the board-walk and reached into the murky water, splashing a bit on his face.

"Careful! Keep your mouth closed." I wasn't sure what was grosser—demon blood or that water. "You could *definitely* catch something. I wouldn't be surprised if your leg spontaneously falls off."

He rose, his lips parted in a chuckle. "Are you a clean freak?"

"Not wanting to wash my face in water that has dead bodies in it hardly gets me clean-freak status."

He gestured to all the demon bodies with his sword. "I'll have you know that I kept all of these bodies out of the water. I'm considerate like that."

I barked a brief laugh, then pointed back to the watery room we'd just come from. "What do you think was in those sarcophagi? No way those things are watertight."

Cade grimaced slightly. "Fair point."

"Exactly." I strode over to the demon bodies that had already started to disappear back to the underworld, grabbed my two daggers, and wiped them on the demon's shirt.

"You're handy with more than just a sword," Cade said.

"If your magic caused catastrophic damage, you'd become handy with weapons, too." I grinned at the memory of bar fights back in Death Valley Junction. "No one likes it if you blow up the best bar in town over a poker disagreement."

"You like poker?"

"I spent my formative years in the closest thing to the Old West. Of course I like poker."

"Hmmm. Maybe a game sometime."

Strip poker.

Nope, nope, nope! Of course my mind went right there, but

my smarter self would not tolerate such shenanigans. If I wanted to keep my distance, strip poker was literally the worst way to go about that.

"Sure, maybe." *Never.* I turned and inspected the rest of the room.

"We will need to talk about your new magic, though," he said.

"Not now." I inspected the rest of the room, but there wasn't much to see. Just the wide, wooden boardwalk that led to heavy wooden doors on the far end of the room. I pointed to them. "Twenty bucks his lair is back there."

"Agreed." Cade strode toward it.

I kept pace with his long strides, my gaze zeroed in on the door. I clutched my daggers, ready for a fight. No way I'd throw a sonic boom down here and risk the church collapsing on us.

We stopped at the wooden doors, and I pressed my ear to one.

"Nothing," I whispered.

Cade nodded, then slowly pushed one open and stuck his head inside. Half a second later, he walked through. I followed.

"Whoa." I whistled low.

The room was empty, like a foyer. We were still in the crypts, with the same arched ceilings and support columns, but the place had been fancied up considerably. Crystal wall sconces shed more light on the space, making it look artistically historic rather than old and creepy. The room was still slightly flooded—maybe two feet of water—but the boardwalk was a beautiful gleaming wood laid with a brilliant red rug. Channels of water ran along either wall and sloshed under the boardwalk.

"Ricketts likes the finer things," Cade said.

"No kidding."

A splashing sound made me turn. I squinted at the water, but saw nothing.

I shook my head. No way there were fish down here. "You hear that?"

"Aye." Cade's brow furrowed. "Let's go. There will be more

126

people down here. I'm not keen on running into them. We need the element of surprise."

"Right. Antidote first, though."

We set off across the boardwalk, crossing under an arch. This room was more like a long hallway, narrower, but with the same wooden boardwalk hovering over the flooded ground.

"He really went to a lot of effort to work underground," I whispered.

"Hardly worth it," Cade said.

The hair stood up on the back of my neck as we made our way deeper into Ricketts's lair. So far it was empty, but it wouldn't stay that way. There were several doors up ahead, and we hurried toward them. Searching every room in this place could take a while.

Footsteps thudded in the distance.

"Someone's coming," I whispered.

"In there." Cade pointed to the closest door.

We darted into the room, which was thankfully empty, and quietly shut the door. I could just barely make out the sounds of footsteps in the distance.

Please don't come in here...

The only light in the room came from the thick gap under the door on either side of the walkway. It'd been channeled out so the water could flow freely. The dim light illuminated the space just enough to make out the boxes that were piled up on the platform that covered almost the entire floor. A two-foot area around the whole thing was open to the water below.

A splash sounded from across the room. Same as before.

I stiffened.

Next to me, Cade turned quietly to face the room, his gaze going straight to where the splash had sounded.

My senses went on high alert as I squinted into the dark. I could barely make out the individual towers of boxes. But something was definitely splashing around.

Two glowing green eyes appeared near the floor.

Something was crawling out of the water!

I raised my blade, hesitating. Waiting to see what the heck it was.

"Shhh," it hissed.

"Shhh?" I whispered back.

"Quiet." It raised a slender arm, putting a finger to its lips. Or at least, where I thought lips would be.

"What is it?" I whispered to Cade.

"No idea."

"Come to help." Its voice was more of a rusty hiss than anything else. Like it wasn't used to talking.

The creature crawled up to us, skinny and almost human shaped, with dark gray skin. The glowing green eyes provided enough light to see its face, and it only appeared sort of human. Long hair hung from its head, looking more like weeds than anything else.

The creature was creepy, but for some reason, I wasn't afraid.

Not because it was small, which it was. No larger than a child. But I felt a strange kinship with it.

"Who are you?" Cade asked.

The creature ignored Cade, its eyes riveted to me, as it crept toward us on its webbed feet and hands.

"Who are you?" Cade repeated.

"I talk to her, the one with the power." Its gaze stayed glued to me.

"I don't have any special power," I said.

"You do, water woman. It is why I speak to you."

Water woman? "Who are you?"

"Squido, of the Kappi clan. We lived here once, my people."

"Kappi? Like Kappa, the water creatures?"

"The Italian branch. This was our home, until he came."

"Ricketts?"

Squido nodded. "Magical obstacles were meant to protect us, but he turned them to his will."

"You mean the rooms with the skeletons and rising water?" I asked.

Squido nodded. "Now he is here, and he built these stupid wooden platforms, and my family is gone."

"Why are you here, then?" I asked.

"To cause problems." The creature grinned, revealing blackened fangs. "I come back to taunt him. I don't like him."

"Me neither."

The creature grinned wider. "Yes. Yes. What do you want here? Only one to come here who doesn't stink of evil." Squido's green gaze darted to Cade. "Him, too, though he's not special like you."

"I'm not special." *Nope! No weird magic to see here, folks!*

Squido shrugged. "What do you want here?"

"To find a potion and to kill Ricketts."

Squido clapped his—or her?—webbed hands together. "Yes. Yes. I will help you. And you will give us back this place."

This was the guide we needed. Squido could get us through this labyrinth. I looked at Cade. "Can we give it back to them?"

Cade frowned, brow furrowed, then he nodded. "Aye. If this is the ancestral homeland of the Kappi clan, we can make that happen."

Squido's eyes glued to me. "How?"

Hmmm. Smart water monster. Squido wanted a plan before we got down to business.

I looked at Cade. "How?"

"If we don't take out all of Ricketts's men, I'll come clean up the rest myself. Then the Protectorate can see about making this a restricted area. A sanctuary protected for the Kappi clan."

I grinned, liking the sound of that. It was like an endangered species preserve, except for water monsters. I looked at Squido. "Satisfied?"

"I trust water woman. You trust him?"

"Yes."

Squido nodded happily, eyes glowing. "Come, come." He waved a webbed hand. "I will help you."

Thank fates for supernaturals who hated Ricketts. They were our biggest asset.

"First, we have to find where he stores his potions. Then we'll go for him," I said.

"Yes, yes." Squido nodded. "We go to the crossroads. Potions to the right. End of the hall. Ricketts's office the other way. To the left. I'll divert guards, you steal and kill."

I winced. He made it sound pretty bad when he said it like that.

Ah well. Beggars couldn't be choosers, and I wasn't going to look a gift monster in the mouth.

The sound of footsteps had faded, so I looked at my companions and said, "Ready to go steal and kill?"

Cade grinned. "Aye."

"Yes, yes!" The water monster gave a little hop of excitement.

"Right, then. Steal and kill." I turned toward the door, wondering what my life had become. It's not like I'd been on the right track before, but *steal and kill* was really off the rails.

CHAPTER NINE

Squido leapt off the platform and swam through the little channel to the right of the door. I looked down into the murky water.

It was just slightly too narrow for me to sneak through that way. And no way Cade could fit.

Thank fates.

I really didn't want to get in that stuff.

We slipped out the door and into the empty hallway. Squido was swimming along the water channel on the left side. He waved at us to follow.

I hurried along on silent feet, glancing into open rooms as we passed. Fortunately, all were empty, save one. And the person in that office was asleep on his desk.

Crime was tiring.

When we neared the crossroads, where the hall dead-ended and split left or right, footsteps sounded from the left.

I stopped dead in my tracks next to Cade, gripping my daggers. Squido darted under the wooden walkway and swam down the left hall. There was a massive splash, then a shout.

We ran for it, peering down the left corridor to see a guard wedged in the narrow water channel on the side of the hall, Squido on top of him, clinging like a monkey. He tore at the guard's neck with his teeth.

There was no screaming—Squido seemed to have gone right for the voice box—and hopefully no one had heard the initial splash and crash.

If that was Squid's signature move, I didn't want to get on his bad side.

I grimaced, then darted right, hurrying along next to Cade. Fortunately, the doors in this hall were all shut, and the one at the end wasn't terribly far away.

Magic seeped out from under the door, a dozen varying signatures.

"Has to be his potions room," I whispered.

Blood Sorcerers performed their magic with blood. They could do some spells, but a lot of what they created was potions and enchanted charms. It wasn't necessarily illegal, though it did walk the line. It all depended on how the blood was obtained. Willingly, and you were good to go.

Unwillingly... Yeah, the Order of the Magica would object.

And knowing Ricketts, I'd bet that he was high on their list.

We stopped at the potions room door, and I pressed my ear to the wood.

"We're good," I whispered, then pushed at the door.

It didn't budge.

"Let me." Cade laid his hand on the wooden door. His magic swelled slightly, and I stepped back, not wanting to get a taste of his death magic again.

It still hit me, sending visions of battle and death into my mind, but magic burst on the air, and the spell that protected the door broke.

He gripped the doorknob, but it didn't turn.

"I got it." I dug into my pocket and pulled out my picks, then got to work. Six seconds later, it popped open.

We stepped inside.

Hundreds of magical signatures rolled out from inside the room. Everything from the scent of clean grass to the taste of old fish. *Ick.*

Tables—cluttered with hundreds of bottles and all sorts of magical tools—lined every wall, and herbs hung from the ceiling.

Before shutting the door, I peered back out at Squido. The body was gone, and so was he. Must have pulled it under the dock.

I shuddered, then shut the door quietly behind us.

The only light came from the dim glow seeping from under the door. Once my eyes adjusted, I hurried to one of the long tables against the wall, going straight for the candlestick.

"Old school." I lit it with a nearby match.

Cade lit one of his own. "Hard to run electric down here, especially if you've stolen the place from some water monsters."

We held our candles near the vials and jars on the tables. They were stacked in wooden boxes and carefully labeled. There were hundreds.

Acid bomb, illusion mist, eternal sunshine, murder, house cat.

"House cat?" I muttered.

"Maybe you turn into one?"

"I don't know." I kinda wanted to take it, though. Just to see.

Get on track!

I bent low over the tables and studied the many little labels. My chest burned with pain as I searched, as if it were urging me on to find the antidote quickly. I tried to breathe shallowly to manage the pain. Thank fates Hedy had given us the pain potion. I couldn't imagine what it'd be like without it.

Cade went to the table along the other wall. A moment later, he stood straight. "Found it."

I hurried over, bending low to inspect the spidery writing that marked the little box full of potions.

LITHICA. Right between JELLY LEGS and SPIDER HEAD.

I poked at the glass bottles in the Lithica box. "There's two different-colored bottles."

"One must be the poison, and the other the antidote."

There was no blue glass, so they hadn't been decanted into bomb form yet. "Only he would know. Good security system. Not great for us."

"Hedy will be able to tell."

"Right, so we take it all." I looked around for a bag.

Footsteps sounded at the door just before it opened. Fear shot through me, cold and bright. I grabbed for the jelly legs potion, going for one with thin glass that was likely to be a bomb—those exploded on impact—then whirled around.

"What are you doing?" An old man stood at the door, face incredulous.

I hurled the jelly legs potion at him.

He collapsed, his legs going out from under him. In his eyes, shock gave way to fear, and he opened his mouth.

Cade was on him before he could scream, slapping a hand over his mouth. Quietly, he shut the door so no one could see us. "Get me a gag."

"On it!" I glanced around frantically, my gaze finally landing on some tape and white cloth. I brought it to Cade, who bound the old man's mouth.

"Now what?" he asked.

"Ahhh, let's call it good." The man was at least seventy years old. His magic stank, a sure sign he didn't use it for good, but... "I can't kill an old man. Just make sure you tie him up good. We'll tell the Order he's here. I'm going to grab the potions."

I took the tape back to the box of Lithica and taped up the top so that the little jars would stay protected inside the wooden box. Then I tossed the whole thing in a large canvas bag I found hanging from a hook on the wall.

"Do one last sweep," I told Cade. "Take anything that looks like it might be an antidote, or anything that looks handy."

I grabbed a box and filled it with a few potions that said ANTI-DOTE, though they didn't say *to what* exactly. But just in case... I didn't want to get this wrong. Then I grabbed a few more potions just for the hell of it. They were usually expensive, and I could use them in a fight.

Sleeping potion, acid bomb, smoke cloud, oil slick, and house cat.

I put the fighting potions into a smaller bag so I could get at them easily, then joined Cade, who was putting another box into the big canvas bag.

"We have to have at least a hundred bottles here," he said.

"Good. One of them has to be the cure. And I like the idea of cleaning Ricketts out."

"Ready to go find him?"

"Born ready." I winced. That sounded way cooler on TV.

Cade grinned at me.

"Whatever. Let's go."

He nodded, kindly letting it slide, and we went to the door. He pushed it open, and I peeked out.

"Coast is clear." I slipped out into the hall, the smaller bag of weaponized potions over my shoulder. Weaponized potions and house cat.

Which could be a weapon. Who was I to say?

I just hadn't been able to resist.

Quickly, we made our way down the hall. My senses were on high alert, listening for footsteps and trying to pick up any unfamiliar magical signatures.

I scanned the water around us, looking for Squido.

A splash sounded from up ahead. A dark gray head popped above the surface of the murky water.

"He's there," I whispered.

Squido pointed to the door at the end of the hall. It had to be the room he'd said would contain Ricketts.

We hurried forward. When we reached the crossroads in the hall, I slowed, pulling a potion bomb out of my little bag. I peered around the edge of the wall, looking down the hall toward the entrance to the catacombs.

"Coast is clear," I murmured.

We moved toward Squido on silent feet.

Then I heard footsteps.

Dang.

I darted back, peering around the corner. A demon was striding toward us. I hurled the potion bomb at him, using all the skill I'd honed while training with my knives.

It crashed against his chest, exploding in a burst of green liquid.

His eyes rolled back in his head, and he keeled over backward, landing hard against the wooden walkway.

He didn't move. Passed out.

I rejoined Cade. "Let's go."

We raced the last twenty feet toward Squido, who'd climbed up onto the walkway and crouched in front of the door at the end of the hall, excitement in his green eyes. He looked a lot like Gollum, but uglier and more charming, if that was possible.

Squido pointed to the door. "Open. Seven inside."

I grimaced. Seven was a lot without using my sonic boom power.

"Where's Ricketts?" I mouthed.

"Straight in. Behind desk." Squido's hiss was low.

"The others?" Cade asked.

"All around room. Sitting."

Cade, who was carrying the bag of antidote potions, took the thing off his shoulder and hung it over a wall sconce, no doubt so it wouldn't get destroyed in the fight that was to come.

I pressed my ear to the door, trying to focus on picking up any voices.

Cade did the same.

Our eyes met.

Tension sent a shiver through me. We were just too close.

Why hadn't he faced the other way?

I dropped my gaze.

"What is it?" a voice growled.

Not Ricketts's. I'd only met him in person once, but his voice wasn't that deep.

"The magic that I need to catch them," Ricketts said.

At least, I thought it was Ricketts.

"How, though?" the lower voice said.

"I must determine that," Ricketts said. "But it's greater power than I've ever known."

I frowned. What the hell was he talking about?

"I don't know, boss," growled the low voice. "You sure you trust her?"

"You leave that to me!"

"All right. All right! Just getting hungry. Making me antsy."

I pulled back from the door. If they were going to come out to eat, we'd lose the element of surprise. Cade drew back as well, clearly thinking the same thing.

Then he pressed his hand to the door. His magic swelled so lightly that I could barely feel it. He turned to me and whispered, "No spell."

Good. "Let's get this show on the road. I hate waiting."

Already, my heart was racing. We needed to get into the battle *now*.

I dug into my bag for a smoke cloud potion and yanked it out. I held it up so Cade could see the label.

He nodded. "On three."

Squido slipped back into the water, no doubt to launch a sneak attack from below. Little did Ricketts know that his stupid walkways had left a secret channel for his enemy.

On three, Cade kicked down the door.

I took a quick look inside—long enough to see Ricketts at the back of the room and three guys on each side—then I hurled the smoke bomb.

137

The little glass ball exploded against the ground. Gray smoke plumed upward, filling the room. The jerks inside began to cough.

Yeah, take that!

He didn't like a taste of his own magic, did he? I wanted to shout it, but that'd give away my position.

I drew my daggers from the ether and rushed into the room, then threw them on memory. There was a thud. A splash. A delighted shriek from Squido.

The second dagger clattered against the wall.

One outta two ain't bad when you can't see.

I crouched low and dug into my sack as Cade rushed toward the side wall, his huge sword drawn. Though I'd normally prefer my sword, in this smoke, I'd have an advantage with the bombs.

Anyway, I liked to mix it up. Adventures in demon slaying. It was important to keep one's work interesting, after all. Variety was the spice of life.

My hand closed around a potion bomb as the smoke in front of me brightened with a yellow glow.

Fireball!

I dove left, skidding low along the ground as the fireball sailed overhead, singing my hair.

"Who are you?" Ricketts bellowed through the smoke.

"Your worst nightmare." *Ah, crap.* That also sounded cooler in the movies.

Whatever.

I dug into my sack for another potion bomb. The smoke was clearing, and I spotted a large form cutting through the gloom. I hurled the potion bomb. The demon dodged, so fast I could hardly see him, and the bomb exploded against the stone wall.

Dang.

Super-fast demons were damned hard to fight. *Sword or bombs?*

Squido leapt from the water behind the demon, catching him

by surprise and clinging to his neck and forehead. He sank his fangs into the demon's skull, and the demon whirled around, trying to grab him.

Bomb it is!

I grabbed a potion bomb and heaved it at the beast. It slammed into his back, exploding in a burst of pink smoke. The demon howled, and the smell of burning flesh rent the air. He tumbled onto his front, Squido going down with him. The little water monster gave another shriek of glee.

Ricketts had climbed onto his desk to get a better vantage point. His long black jacket flapped around him, making him look like a *Matrix* wannabe. His dark hair and goatee were ruthlessly trimmed, and his black eyes blazed.

A hulking demon stood in front of him, guarding his master.

To the left, Cade was fighting the only other demon. The beast was eight and a half feet tall if he was an inch and wielded a blade as long as I was. Squido was still on top of his demon, chowing away.

I grimaced, turning my gaze back to Ricketts, who looked enraged.

"Hiding behind your hired gun? Afraid to fight?" I taunted.

Ricketts grinned. Shark-like. "I have you right where I want you. After all that effort, you came right to me!"

"Where? Perfectly in line to kick your ass?" I dug into my sack.

He hurled a potion bomb. I dived left, and it sailed by me. The glass ball exploded against the wall, and a plume of white mist unfurled. I lunged away from it, toward Ricketts. It was the only direction to go to get away.

But the mist caught me in its grip, clinging tight to my legs. I tried to run, but its grip held tight. Like the blob from that movie.

I threw the potion bomb in my hand.

It crashed into the chest of the big demon, and surprise flashed on his face.

"What, thought my arms were caught, too?" I asked.

Light swirled around the demon and he shrank, turning into a white house cat with piercing blue eyes.

I looked at Ricketts. "Seriously, an *actual* house cat?"

I couldn't kill a freaking kitty. Even if it was a demon. The cat hissed and ran behind the desk.

Well, that was one way to get rid of enemies. But I really hoped he'd turn back into a demon. I did *not* have time to find a home for a magical demon cat.

On the other side of the room, Cade continued to battle the huge demon, landing a good blow to the side. They were evenly matched, both bleeding from wounds to their arms and chest. It might be a while.

I pulled my sword from the ether as Ricketts dug into the pocket of his flowing coat. He pulled out another potion bomb.

Shit.

I swung the sword for the mist that surrounded me, hoping I could cut through the stuff. Ricketts chucked his bomb. I dodged as best I could, but with my legs trapped, I couldn't go far.

The acid bomb nailed me in the shoulder.

I shrieked as the pain tore through me. "Bastard!"

"I'll take that as a compliment."

I hacked at the mist surrounding my legs. The grip loosened, until finally, I slipped free.

Ricketts dug into his pocket, then flung another potion bomb. I dove left, avoiding the bomb but not the backsplash. The thing exploded against the wall, spraying me with a freezing cold solution that burned my skin.

"I haven't tested that one yet," Ricketts said. "What's the verdict?"

"That you're a two-bit egg sucking rat bastard." I scrambled to my feet.

I lunged for him, sword raised.

He stuck his hand into his pocket, but before he could pull

anything out, the desk beneath him rocked, rising up from the ground and throwing him off it.

Right into me.

I collapsed under him, but not before my sword sliced his arm. He hissed and rolled off me.

Behind him, the big demon who'd turned into a house cat climbed out from behind the upended desk. The spell had worn off while he'd been hiding under it.

Cade landed a killing blow to his massive demon—a stab right to the neck—then leapt for the demon who was no longer fabulously fluffy.

I scrambled to my feet and raised my sword, going for Ricketts.

He threw a potion bomb to the ground in front of him. It exploded and magic surged up, a pearlescent shield. My sword collided with it.

"Ah, ah, ah." Ricketts gave an evil smirk. "Not through my shield."

"I'll just wait it out. Or Cade might get you."

"He won't. But I will get you." His eyes glittered with promise.

"Pretty hard to get me when you're outnumbered." Behind him, Cade beheaded the last demon. "And yep, there goes your last guard."

"Oh, there's more than one way to get you. And now I have the means," he hissed. Then he threw something on the ground.

I caught sight of a black pebble right before a silvery cloud burst up.

"No!" I screamed, lunging for him.

I slammed into the barrier, getting a miserable electric shock for the trouble. Pain surged.

He stepped into the transportation charm and disappeared.

"Damn it!" I nearly threw my sword to the ground, but I'd *never* do that. No amount of frustration would make me let go of my weapon. But it was close. "Damn it, damn it, damn it!"

Squido looked up from his demon, who'd almost entirely disappeared. "Missed?"

"Yes." I scowled. "But we'll get him, Squido. I promise."

Squido nodded. "You'd better."

Cade wiped his blade off on one of the demon's shirts. "Are there any more in the building, Squido?"

"I think not. But more may come. He has more."

"We'll take care of them." Cade looked toward me. His chest and arms seeped blood, but otherwise, he looked as dashing as an ancient Celtic warrior. Which he was, basically. Except for the ancient part. "Are you all right?"

"Yeah." I stepped toward him, then immediately stumbled. "Okay, no."

Adrenaline had kept me going, but now I was starting to feel my wounds. The acid bite on my shoulder, in particular.

Concern darkened Cade's features and he approached, studying my shoulder. "The acid has stopped eating your flesh, at least."

"You really know how to soothe a girl."

"Sorry. But your leather jacket protected you." His gaze met mine. "Let me heal you."

"You can heal?"

"It's the other side of the battle power. Wounding and healing. That gives my power balance. I don't use it often, though."

"Wow." That sounded great, but... "It's not that bad. Let's get out of here and deal with it. I don't want Ricketts coming back with reinforcements. We really only had a chance when we had the element of surprise. And we need to get these antidotes to Hedy so she can identify the proper one."

"I'll call Emily, the transport mage. She can meet us at the safe house."

I nodded, then turned toward Squido. "Can you lead us out of here so we don't get drowned or destroyed by skeletons?"

Squido nodded. "Yes, yes. Come."

We followed him out of the room. Cade grabbed the bag of antidotes from where he'd stashed it, then we headed down the boardwalk. Though there wasn't supposed to be anyone here, my senses were on high alert.

I couldn't wait to get out of this underwater death trap.

When we reached the crossroads in the hall—one direction leading out, the other leading to the potions room—I stopped and looked at Cade. "You think we can clean him out in sixty seconds?"

He nodded.

"Good." I looked at Squido. "Hang on a moment."

We ran to the potion room. The man was still bound in the corner.

"I'll send someone down to pick him up," Cade said. "We'll give him to the Order."

"Good." I didn't like the idea of killing non-demons. Even bad ones.

We grabbed up several large sacks and filled them with as many potions as they would hold. Probably got ninety percent of the stash. Call me greedy, but I liked the idea of cleaning him out. It'd also give him less weapons.

My shoulder burned as we carried our booty back to Squido, who waited for us.

"Good." He nodded, then turned and hurried down the hall.

It didn't take long to make it back, not with Squido knowing just how to get us through the enchantments.

At the stairs, Squido said goodbye.

"We'll take care of the rest," I promised, meeting Cade's gaze.

He nodded.

"Good." Squido waved, and we hurried up through the quiet church.

"Where now?" I asked once we made it out onto the front steps of the church.

"I'll find out." He pulled a cell phone from his pocket, then gestured for me to follow.

We hurried through the narrow, darkened streets of Venice. I listened as he talked to someone—presumably someone from the Protectorate—and made arrangements to meet.

He hung up as we reached the speedboat, and carefully lowered his sacks of potion bombs into the cockpit. I did the same with mine.

We hopped in, and he pulled away from the dock, the engine at a low rumble.

"How are those wounds?" he asked.

"Fine." They burned like hell, actually, but I wasn't going to complain. Wouldn't do any good, anyway.

The moon hung heavy and full in the sky, glittering on the canals.

"We're going to a Protectorate safe house," he said. "Emily, the transporter, will meet us there."

"The transporter?"

"Yes. She'll take the potions back so that Hedy can determine the cure."

"Perfect." We'd lose very little time that way.

The smaller back canals were dead silent as we motored through the town, passing historic buildings with baskets full of flowers tumbling from the windows. Despite the quietness of the back canals, the Grand Canal was still bustling with party life. People in costume were singing and dancing.

I slouched low in the seat, not wanting anyone to see how beat up I was. I didn't know how alert the cops were here, but we didn't need to get caught by humans. Any delay was unwelcome, since I was beyond ready for some dinner and a shower. And maybe a bit of that healing Cade had promised.

When he pulled the boat up to a massive white mansion at the edge of the Grand Canal, I looked at him. "You have *got* to be kidding me."

CHAPTER TEN

"Not a joke." He pulled the boat into the garage—boathouse?—that was on the first level of the four-story mansion.

"This is really the Protectorate's safe house? One of the biggest mansions in Venice?"

"Aye. Ricketts may send his goons after you, but they won't get through here." He cut the engine and tied the boat off to the dock, then climbed out. He reached a hand down.

I took it with my good arm and let him haul me up, then helped him gather the bags out of the boat. I followed him to the stairs, wincing as the protective magic prickled over my skin.

"Let me go first," he said. "The magic will recognize me and disengage."

I swept an arm out. "Age before beauty."

He chuckled, then disengaged the charm locking the door and started up the stairs. We passed the first three floors entirely. By the third flight, I was panting, exhausted from the day's endeavors.

"These floors are empty," he said. "Security."

"What kind?"

"Statues that come alive on the first floor, poison gas on the second floor, and giant snakes on the third—they're just magic though. Otherwise, it'd be inhumane."

"Snakes don't like mansions in Venice." I nodded sagely. At least, I was aiming for sagely. "Everyone knows that."

"Precisely."

I grinned, liking how he went along with my silliness. It was the only thing keeping me from tearing up over the pain in my shoulder.

He let us onto the fourth floor, disengaged another locked door, and my mouth immediately watered at the scent of pizza. The lights were already on, illuminating an amazing living area that looked like something out of a fancy old movie.

"Took you long enough." Emily grinned, stepping forward out of the living room, which was done entirely in cream and pale gold. Several pizza boxes sat on the table. "Brought you food."

"Thank you," Cade said.

"You're a saint." I beelined straight for her, handing over the box containing the antidotes. "The cure is one of the potions in here, but Hedy will have to test them. And seriously, thank you for the pizza."

She nodded, and I didn't waste any time, leaving her to chat with Cade while I went for the pizza. I chowed down on pepperoni, trying not to pay attention to my arm or the pain in my chest.

I prayed that Hedy could identify that antidote soon.

"See you later!" Emily called. Then she disappeared.

I swallowed the last bite of my third piece of pizza as Cade joined me. I gestured to the fancy room, and the huge arched windows that gave a view of the Grand Canal. "The Protectorate sure likes it fancy."

"Not always. But when in Rome... Or Venice." He sat next to me, his big form taking up a good bit of sofa real estate. He leaned in to inspect my arm and shoulder. "It still looks bad. Can I do something about it?"

"Like what exactly?" I swallowed hard. He was so close that I could see the different colors of green in his eyes, the small muscles and veins in his hands. Against all odds, he still smelled good.

Heat flushed through me.

"My healing power is the opposite of death. I'd give you a small amount of my power. Of life. And your wounds would disappear. It's a last resort, something I do rarely."

"Um, okay." I shifted so that my shoulder was near him.

He raised a big hand and hovered it over the acid burn. He was even closer now. So close I could just lean in and kiss him.

I hadn't been attracted to someone in ages. And Cade was... well, a freaking war god. And as handsome and strong as you'd expect one to be. I swallowed hard, trying to focus on anything else.

Then his power began to flow into me, strong and bright. I gasped. It filled me with light. With warmth. And I felt him.

Not physically, but who he was. Like, the qualities that made him unique.

Bravery, honor, pure goodness. A little bit of danger and ruthlessness. Each quality felt slightly different but was so distinct.

Then heat ran through me, shivering along my skin and into my bones.

Desire welled up.

His for me? Or mine for him?

My gaze darted to his. The green of his eyes blazed with warmth, his lids slightly lowered. His full lips parted.

Warmth surged through me. The pain had faded from my body, and pure *want* had taken its place.

His gaze dropped to my lips. He gripped the edge of the table tightly, his knuckles turning white. The one that hovered in front of my shoulder trembled slightly.

Oh fates. Did he want to kiss me?

From the heat in his gaze—*yes.*

I leaned in slightly, more of a sway than a conscious movement.

He swallowed hard and removed his hand that hovered over shoulder. "It's better."

The spell broke. The connection severed.

I gasped, leaning backward. The heat was still there, the desire. But the connection was gone. I almost vibrated with the loss.

Had he really wanted to kiss me? Why hadn't he?

Not that it mattered. *Get it together.*

Finally, I composed myself. "What happened there?"

His brow creased. "That's unusual."

"I could feel you."

"Me too."

"Really?" My heart thundered. "What did you find?"

"Honor and love. Fear and bravery."

"Fear?" My gaze snapped to his.

"Aye. I could sense it back in the crypt, too. Anytime we were about to face a new challenge. But then you'd throw yourself right into it."

"Well, yeah. Of course I was scared. I'm not a freaking idiot. I've got a highly developed sense of self-preservation."

"But you jumped into the fight anyway." His green gaze searched mine, assessing.

The heat still hadn't faded, but the strangeness of talking about myself on such a...a personal level, was starting to drive it off.

"Why'd you jump in if you were so afraid?"

"Gotta get the job done."

"So as soon as you get scared, you leap into the fray."

"Yeah. I'm like Pavlov's dog now. Scared, fight. Scared, fight." I shrugged. "It's worked out well for me so far."

"I'd say so." He nodded, eyebrows raised and his expression clearly impressed. "I've been with many people in battle. Thousands. Not just what I've seen myself, but a sense I get. Like I've known all the warriors who've ever lived. Many of them lack fear."

"Ha, well, not me."

"That's what makes you braver than most."

Heat singed my cheeks. "Let's change the subject."

"All right." His gaze sharpened. "You developed new magic back in the tomb."

"Actually, let's talk about how brave I am."

His keen gaze pinned me like a bug. I swallowed hard, the heat inside me intensifying into a searing discomfort.

I was majorly attracted to a guy I couldn't trust.

Sure he was honorable, but where did that honor lie?

Not with me. He barely knew me.

And sure, the Protectorate said they wanted me and Ana, but would they still want us when they learned what we were? They wanted our skills and power, but they didn't know where that magical power came from. Even we didn't know that. But my mother had sure put the fear of discovery into us.

"Bree. You can tell me." His deep voice was soothing.

Except that it did just the opposite for me. "Not much to tell."

"You have serious power. Magic that you need to learn to control."

"I will."

"I understand that you're wary," he said. "I'll help you."

"Okay." *Yeah, right.*

"I mean it."

"Hmmm hmmm." I stood and wandered over to the window, knowing that I was blowing this. I wasn't doing a good job at deflecting his interest or attention, but I wasn't used to having a real conversation with anyone besides Ana. Or Rowan, when she'd been around.

The rest of our life was fighting and bullshitting with our

clients. This 'up close and personal' stuff was like a dog trying to speak English. And I was the dog.

"You should eat. The pizza is getting cold." I pushed open the window and leaned out, sucking in the warm, fresh air.

The sight below was breathtaking—the wide Grand Canal stretched out in both directions, moonlight glittering on the water. Huge mansions lit by golden light loomed on either side, and colorful boats floated below.

It'd be really romantic if I weren't scared for my life. And Ana's.

That was my priority right now. Then figuring out if we'd stay at the Protectorate. I was scared of revealing what I really was, but I was also scared of my new powers.

So, which was more frightening?

I had no idea.

I turned back to Cade.

He was eating a slice of pizza and watching me, a ridiculous activity that he somehow managed to make look sexy.

Oh, I was an idiot.

"We need to figure out where Ricketts went," I said. "If he has another bolt hole."

Cade nodded. "We will. But first, we'll rest. You look like you're about to fall over."

I felt like it, too. But now that an antidote had been found, the worst of our time crunch had passed. "Okay. Tomorrow we'll get started." I turned and inspected the large room. "Which way to a bedroom?"

He pointed left, to a doorway near the windows. "Take that one. There are women's clothes in the armoire. And I'll see you in the morning."

I nodded, not bothering to say goodnight, then turned and headed to the bedroom.

I flicked on the light, getting a glimpse of a bedroom that

looked like something a king would sleep in—all ivory and gold again—and immediately headed for the bed.

I barely made it out of my dirty clothes before falling face-first onto the downy mattress. As I drifted off, images of Cade flashed through my mind, along with snippets of the conversation I'd heard through the door at Ricketts's headquarters.

~

Hours later, I shot awake, heart pounding
I know where Ricketts is.

CHAPTER ELEVEN

The conversation that I'd heard through the door had been running through my head all night. Finally, I'd put it together. In a dream, maybe?

I leapt out of bed and raced across the room, realizing right before I hit the door that I was nearly naked. I grabbed a blanket that had been thrown over a chair near the window and threw it over my shoulders, then burst out into the living room.

"Cade!" I shouted. "Get up!"

There were four doors leading off the main living area. Which was his?

I ran toward the one directly across from me. Right before I reached it, he pulled open the door and stepped out. I nearly collided with his naked chest.

If I hadn't been so freaked out, I'd have taken a moment to admire his godlike muscles. And since he was a god, I wouldn't have been embarrassed about describing him as godlike.

"What is it?" His dark hair was mussed from sleep.

"I know where Ricketts is."

"Really?" His eyes sharpened, any last vestiges of sleepiness disappearing.

"Yeah. He said there was more than one way to get to me. He meant my sister." The loss of her would be worse than my own death.

Ricketts must have known that.

"Back at his compound, we heard him through the door. He was talking about magic that would finally allow him to capture us. Someone gave it to him. His goons haven't been successful, so I haven't worried too much about them. But *he* would be. Now he has something that will help him try to nab us directly."

"And since he's failed with you, he'll try for her." Cade nodded, his face serious. "That makes sense. We'll go to her immediately. She's in a safe house in northeast Scotland. A castle in the woods with excellent security. Don't worry. There will be over a dozen guards around the property, ready to apprehend Ricketts or his men. And there are more in the castle with her."

"A trap. Good." I turned to go back to the bedroom to get dressed. "Let's get out of here soon. Do we have a transport charm to get to Syre?"

"Syre? I didn't say where she was located. How did you know?"

I turned. "We have our own connection charms. We bought them a while ago." After Rowan had disappeared. If only we'd done it sooner. "Family is everything, Cade."

His gaze shuttered slightly.

Hmm. Did he no longer have a family?

That was a question for another time.

I hurried back toward the bedroom and got dressed in record time, digging through the assortment of spare clothes in the armoire. I found jeans, a T-shirt, and a leather jacket that suited me, then returned to the living room.

Cade was dressed and ready to go, wearing clothes that were identical to his last ones.

"You keep things stored here?" I asked.

"In all the safe houses." He pulled a black stone out of his pocket. "Ready?"

"Yeah." I joined him and took his hand.

He threw the stone on the ground, and a plume of sparkling gray smoke rose up. We stepped into it, appearing in the woods in Scotland a moment later.

Into chaos.

Panicked shouts echoed through the forest. My heart leapt into my throat, and I spun around, searching for the threat. The morning sun filtered through the trees, illuminating the broken branches and trunks that had been snapped in half.

"He's here!" I drew my throwing knives from the ether and raced for Ana, drawn by the tug in my chest.

Cade joined me, his long legs carrying him ahead of me.

The destruction of the woods was crazy—huge trees torn up and toppled over. Broken branches and gouges in the dirt. Something catastrophic had torn through here. A body lay about fifteen feet off the path of destruction. A man.

I didn't stop, though guilt tugged at me.

But I could feel Ana. She was here. I had to get to her.

The forest lightened as I neared the edge. People were leaping out of the trees and joining me on the path, running for the castle ahead. Some looked familiar, like Protectorate staff. They must've been the guards.

"What happened?" I screamed at a nearby man.

He was blond, and his magic smelled of the sea. His gaze looked wild. "Tornado."

In *Scotland*?

That was insane.

I sprinted out of the forest. In the middle of the clearing sat a tall stone tower surrounded by a hulking castle wall.

A chunk was torn out of the wall, and a large gray tornado was sweeping off into the distance.

Then Ana disappeared.

I felt it, deep in my chest, and stumbled, going to my knees.

She was no longer here. And the tornado was gone, too.

No! I scrambled to my feet, heart thundering.

The sun shone brightly on the mountains sweeping out in front of me. They were coated with purple heather, a beautiful sight if not for the chaos of the wounded castle and the people running around, shouting for their colleagues.

I ran for the castle, for answers. For Cade.

I found him at the edge of the wall, staring through the giant hole that had been torn by the tornado. The castle inside was a single tower with walls at least ten feet thick. It was easy to get exact dimensions since the danged corner of the castle was missing too.

Near the castle wall, Hedy was on the phone. Possibly with the Protectorate? Jude ran out of the castle, scrambling over the broken stone. Her gray hair was coated with dust, and the stone-cold expression that I'd first seen her wearing was replaced with panic.

"I've never seen anything like it!" She ran up to us, panting. "He came as a tornado! Blasted through twenty of our guards before we realized what was happening."

"Did he get Ana?" Cade demanded.

"Yes. He got her." I turned on Jude, voice harsh. "You said she'd be safe here! But she was bait. And she was caught."

"I'm sorry." Jude's expression hardened. "He shouldn't have had weather magic like that. *No one* has weather magic like that."

"Someone gave him more power, but I have no idea who," I said. "It just happened, though. We heard him talking about it in Venice."

"Damn it." A thundercloud crossed Jude's face.

"Bree, can you locate where your sister went?" Cade asked.

I frowned, focusing on the connection charm that I hoped would help me find Ana. I stepped back from everyone, trying to clear my mind. *This* was why we'd bought these things. So we wouldn't lose another sister. I couldn't bear to lose another sister. Tears pricked my eyes.

Please work.

If Ricketts knew that she had a connection charm, he could do something to block it. Fear chilled my skin.

Please don't realize.

"What's she doing?" Jude asked Cade.

"Give her a moment."

I envisioned Ana, begging the connection charm to make a link. Finally, it flared to life inside me. I looked up. "Mexico. A hundred miles east of Mexico City. That's where he's taken her."

Jude nodded, her expression firm and accepting. "Fine. We'll send reinforcements with you." Her gaze met Cade's. "How many transport charms do you have?"

"Three more."

Jude nodded. "Good. That will transport fifteen people. Emily can take more."

Hedy hurried up to us. "Bree. Your sister has had her antidote." She dug into her pocket and handed me a little vial. "Here's yours. Take it before you go."

"Thank fates." At least that was fixed.

I looked down at the vial. Did I trust her?

For so long, I'd trusted no one but Ana. But Ana had trusted Hedy enough to take the potion.

And I *did* trust Hedy. Even though it was strange to admit to myself.

Bottoms up.

I drank the potion, then shivered as strength flowed through me. The pain in my chest faded, a glorious pleasure. I hadn't realized how crappy I'd been feeling. I'd chalked up any weakness to exhaustion, but it'd been the poison.

"Thanks. I feel a lot better."

"Bree!" A feminine voice sounded from behind me.

I turned.

Caro ran for me, Ali, and Haris at her side.

"We were in the woods, guarding the castle. I'm sorry he got past us."

"He had magic none of us anticipated. Something huge."

"Let's go get her," Caro said. "We've got your back."

My chest warmed. No one had ever said that to me except Rowan and Ana. "Thanks."

"Where are we off to?" Ali grinned. "I've been itching for a fight."

"Mexico."

Cade joined me, resting a big hand on my shoulder. It was stupid, but I drew strength from it. Behind Caro, a crowd gathered. About twenty of them.

Our reinforcements.

Maybe this Protectorate thing wasn't so bad after all. Not if they had our backs like this.

"I have three charms," Cade said. "Divide into groups of five. Three will take the charms, Emily will take the rest." He turned to me. "We'll go first with Emily and get the coordinates. Then she'll return and tell everyone else where to go."

"Perfect."

Cade handed the charms over to Jude, and Emily joined us.

"Ready?" She held out her hands.

Cade and I each took one.

"Imagine where we're going," she said. "Picture it in your mind as clearly as you can. I'll take us there."

"Okay." I did as she asked, feeling the location more than seeing it. But there was water and jungle, the sound of night animals. Moonlight.

A moment later, the ether sucked us in. My heart thundered as we stepped out into the dark night.

In front of us, the moon hung heavy over an island in the middle of a calm lagoon. A massive step pyramid sat in the middle of the island, surrounded on all sides by smaller pyramids.

"Texochtatlan," Cade breathed. He tore his gaze away and looked at his fancy watch, pressing some buttons. He looked up at Emily and rattled off some numbers.

Coordinates, I realized.

She nodded and disappeared. Cade's awed gaze returned to the abandoned ancient city.

"What is it?" I asked.

"The capital of the supernatural Aztecs. Human Aztecs built Tenochtitlan, which is now in Mexico City. It was much like this. But this one is too far into the jungle. Humans have never found it."

"Aztecs?" *Shit.* Back when we'd still had a TV, before Rowan had disappeared and we'd spent all our spare money hunting for her, we'd loved old history shows. "Didn't they practice human sacrifice? *Blood* sacrifice?"

Cade's gaze turned dark. "They did."

My heart almost burst out of my chest, and fear iced my skin. "Oh no. That's what's changed. The reason he's upped his game in trying to catch us. He's not just going to kill us. He wants more than that. Magic. Our blood."

"Aye. This is no coincidence."

I sucked in a ragged breath and started forward. No time to delay.

The lagoon was about fifty meters from us. A long bridge, at least a hundred meters in length, stretched over it. Several more bridges spanned the lagoon on other sides. The full moon gleamed on the massive pyramid in the middle of the island. It had a wide, flat top and was built of huge steps, unlike the Egyptian pyramids that were smooth sided.

We were too far away to see people, but Ana was definitely here. I could feel her.

"It's been abandoned for centuries," Cade said. "The supernatural Aztecs lasted longer than the human ones since the conquistadors never found them, but they left here long ago."

My gaze raced over the bridge and the city beyond. It was magical, in an ancient kind of way. I could just imagine the ceremonies they'd once had here.

"Badass," a voice murmured from beside me.

I turned to see Ali, his gaze wide. Haris and Caro stood next to him, along with Jude and another man I didn't recognize. I spun, catching sight of about fifteen more people behind us.

Everyone was here.

"Let's go." I started for the bridge, Cade at my side.

"We've got this," Caro murmured.

I hoped so. Without Ana…

There'd be nothing.

I stepped on the stone bridge, and a vibration of magic sang up my leg. I looked up at Cade. "Be ready for anything."

"I feel it," he murmured.

I drew my throwing daggers and jogged across the bridge. On either side, the water gleamed murkily in the moonlight. As we neared the middle, the magic in the air became stronger. A fierce prickle that made my hair stand on end.

Protective charms.

Nearby, the water splashed. I jumped, whirling. Everyone stopped in their tracks, frozen.

The water splashed again, big enough that it could actually be the freaking kraken.

Then a monster burst forth, mouth gaping wide with serrated teeth gleaming in the moonlight. It hurtled for the bridge, cutting through the water with unnatural speed. It looked like a giant monster frog, a demon from the depths.

"Cueyatl," Cade said. "Mythical Aztec beast."

"How do they think up these things?" It should have been kinda silly, but instead, it was freaking terrifying. And my measly weapons wouldn't do any good against something of this size.

159

The beast crouched in the water, eyeing us from twenty feet away. Gauging the distance for its next jump?

I shuddered, then dug into my satchel and pulled out a random potion bomb, then hurled it at the beast. It exploded in its mouth, a plume of blue smoke rising into the air.

Nothing happened. *Crap!*

Someone heaved a massive fireball, but it, too, was devoured by the monster. Caro's deadly water jets bounced off the beast.

Then the thing was on us, leaping through the air with its jaws open wide. Its gaping maw was so big, it could swallow me without chewing.

We threw ourselves to the ground. The beast sailed overhead, water and slime dripping coldly onto our backs. A loud splash sounded from the other side of the bridge.

I scrambled to my feet, leaning over. It was turning around, making a big circle to try again.

"It devours our magic," Cade said.

"Could be growing stronger," Caro added.

My mind raced, heart thundering. The water called to me, a living thing that I could feel as if it were an extension of myself. I had no freaking clue if it would work, but…

Not like I had a lot of options.

I called to the murky water, feeling every molecule and envisioning it rising up, forming a great wave. It did as I commanded, water sucking back from the shore and gathering underneath the giant fanged frog, picking it up like a boat on the sea.

"Back!" I screamed, and the water flowed away from the bridge, carrying the beast with it.

The monster leapt from the mounded wave, but I forced more water at it, catching it in mid-leap and carrying it away.

Then I turned and ran, desperate to get off the damned death bridge.

Ahead of us, a dozen war cries rent the night. Warriors burst from the ground, ghostly gray figures of muscular men and women wearing feathered headdresses and carrying spears.

Their blazing blue eyes landed on us, and they charged.

Shit. There had to be over thirty of them.

The bridge was only wide enough for two at a time. They charged onto it, footsteps thundering as they waved their spears and shouted.

Even with my new charm, my sonic boom might destroy the bridge and send us into the water with the Cueyatl, so that was definitely out. I couldn't bet everyone's lives on it working.

Though they were a ghostly gray color, they looked solid. I prayed weapons would work.

I hurled one dagger, then another, striking two in the chest. They stumbled and fell. Their companions leapt over them.

"Duck!" Caro screamed.

I ducked low. Water streamed over my head, spearing through the chests of two ancient warriors. They tumbled back into their compatriots, but were soon overrun.

"Trade me," Cade shouted.

Caro joined me in the front, shooting her deadly water spouts while I dug into my pouch full of potion bombs. A big part of me really liked using Ricketts's own magic against him.

I hurled the bombs at the warriors, lighting one on fire and coating another with acid. They both leapt into the lake. Caro took out the next two, but there was an endless stream of them.

The rest were nearly upon us now, only five feet away.

"Switch!" Caro yelled.

Cade took her place. I drew a shield and my sword. He drew his.

And we collided with the warriors, blocking with our shields, slicing through their wooden spears, and jabbing with our blades. In the tight quarters, I remained keenly aware of Cade.

Last thing I needed was to take out my backup.

Finally, we reached the end of the bridge, spilling into a mass of the warriors. But at least we had more room to fight.

I called upon my sonic boom power, throwing it out in front of me to clear a path. It exploded, bowling over a dozen of the fighters.

"Go!" I raced through the opening, headed for the massive pyramid in front of us.

Ana was up there. I could feel it.

Cade stayed close by my side. I sprinted full out, determined to get past the warrior guards. A quick glance behind showed that they'd closed back around our fellow fighters. The Protectorate was holding their own, though, keeping the warriors occupied while Cade and I ran for the pyramid.

On either side, smaller pyramids dotted the path. But it was the enormous one, at least three hundred feet tall, that we needed to reach.

The moon was getting low. Dawn was near.

Was Ricketts waiting for dawn? Many ancient sacrifices had been timed around the sun.

I sprinted faster, trying to ignore the magic that prickled at my skin. As we neared the pyramid, I thought that maybe I could make out the figures on top. There were more on the stairs, about a quarter of the way up the pyramid.

Two of them. Guards.

"Watch out!" I screamed.

The figure on the right, his cloak whipping in the wind, raised his hands. Magic exploded on the air.

The ground beneath my feet rose up. He was controlling the earth!

I leapt off the rising ground, stumbling onto flat earth, then kept running. I had to get close enough to throw a sonic boom or potion bomb. We were still so far away.

The figure on the left hurled a bolt of lightning at us. It cracked, loud in the night, and the flash made my vision go.

Blindly, I dove left, skidding on the ground and narrowly avoiding the strike. Then the earth began to rise beneath me.

My heart thundered as I scrambled to my feet and ran across the rising earth, leaping over loose gravel and trying to find the steadiest parts. When I reached the edge, it had risen over eight feet in the air.

Cade ran below me, having avoided the rising earth.

I took a running leap, trying to break my fall by rolling. Pain sang up through my leg as the ground tore at my skin, but I managed to make it to my feet and keep running.

A lightning bolt shot right at Cade, but he dodged, leaping aside. Then his round shield appeared on his arm. He heaved back, then hurled the thing at the mage.

It sliced off his head. He flew backward, crashing into the pyramid and lying still.

The shield turned in the air. The earth mage roared, throwing out his hands. Again, the earth began to rumble and rise. But the shield silenced that mage, too, taking off his head just as neatly.

"Nice." I gasped, running as fast as I could toward the pyramid.

Sweat poured down my face. The sky began to lighten. Dawn was definitely coming.

Finally, after what felt like ages of running, we reached the edge of the pyramid.

More than a thousand normal steps led upward, a staircase cutting through the large stone ledges that made up the major steps of the pyramid.

My lungs already burned and my heart felt like it was about to explode, but I began to climb, racing as quickly as I could. What I wouldn't give for the buggy right now. Those wheels could tear right up these stairs.

"Go ahead of me!" I shouted. He was so much faster.

He nodded and ran, but only made it up a short way before the stone ledges on either side of him began to shift.

A stone jaguar leapt out of the pyramid, charging for him. He returned his sword to the ether, and then brilliant silver light swirled around him.

A second later, the huge wolf stood in his place, then lunged for the jaguar. They collided in a mass of fangs and claws, wrestling on the stairs.

Holy crap.

Still pretty insane to witness.

I ran past them as Cade grappled with the cat, leaving him and the rest of the Protectorate behind. As the sun rose, it was just me.

Running out of time.

I was halfway up the pyramid when an ear-piercing shriek rent the air, chilling my skin. I looked toward the sky, gasping when I caught slight of the winged snake. It was huge. White feathers decorated its wings, and green scales gleamed in the low light of gloaming.

The snake dove for me, hurtling through the sky. I lunged away from its gaping jaws, barely avoiding a bloody death. The creatures swooped high into the sky, diving back to take another shot.

I called upon my sonic boom power, grateful as hell to have this magic.

But he needed to be close, so I could ensure he was hit with the hardest part of the blast. He was so big I'd have to throw everything at him.

I waved my arms. "Come and get me!"

He hurtled toward me, mouth gaping to reveal gleaming white fangs as long as my arm. My heart leapt into my throat as I powered up my magic.

Come on, come on!

He was nearly on me, so close that I could smell his fetid breath.

With a scream, I threw my magic at the beast, using the charm to help my accuracy.

The sonic boom tore through the night, slamming into the monster and sending him tumbling through the sky. *Thank fates!*

I spun, sprinting for the top of the pyramid. The sky was now red as fire, the dawn sun lighting up the ancient ceremonial site.

When I reached the platform at the top, my lungs burned and sweat poured down my face. I gasped, taking in the scene.

Ana was tied to a pillar, wind whipping her blonde hair away from her face. Ricketts stood in front of her, a gleaming black dagger raised. Red sunlight glinted on the blade.

"*Nooooo!*" I ran for them, hoping my scream would distract.

Ricketts jerked, then brought the blade down.

Right into Ana's flesh.

CHAPTER TWELVE

Rage and fear filled me to bursting as I sprinted for them.

Ricketts whirled around, his dagger dripping blood. His black coat whipped in the wind, and his eyes gleamed with power. "Good! You're here."

I reached into my satchel and hurled a potion bomb at him. He dodged it, rolling to the ground.

Ana thrashed against her bonds, blood pouring down her shoulder.

Thank fates.

Not a fatal blow.

Ricketts rose to his feet, glowering at me. "You use my own magic against me?"

"Duh." I grabbed another potion bomb. "I like the poetic nature of it."

He reached into the pocket of his long black coat and withdrew a round glass vial. But instead of hurling it at me, he threw it to the ground.

I lunged for him, afraid he'd run again. But instead, a great orange cloud of fire burst up from the ground. Ricketts waved an arm toward me, and the flame rushed forward.

I hurled a sonic boom toward the flame, but it sailed right through. *Crap!*

That *never* happened. Fire always exploded against my sonic boom. But not Ricketts's crazy fire.

I dove low, covering my head. The fire blazed over me, singing my back.

I leapt up, drawing one of my daggers from the ether and hurling it at Ricketts. He dodged, but it plunged into his shoulder.

He howled.

Good. Tit for tat. Just like he'd given Ana.

I raised my other blade, but before I could throw it, he shoved something into his mouth. A half second later, the air turned gray around him, swirling until he turned into a tornado.

Crap!

The thing was huge, roaring in the quiet dawn. This was the new magic he'd been given.

It thundered toward me, tearing across the top of the pyramid. My heart thundered wildly as I called on my magic, throwing the biggest sonic boom I could manage.

It cracked loudly in the air and crashed into the tornado, disrupting the wind pattern. The thing exploded, throwing a human Ricketts off his feet.

"Ana!" I ran for her, drawing my sword.

She grinned, her face creased with pain and her shoulder pouring blood. "Bree!"

"I gotcha." I sliced the bindings at her back, and she tumbled forward.

I tried to wrap an arm around her waist, but she pushed me off. "We gotta fight."

She grimaced, then threw out one of her protective shields as Ricketts rose to his feet.

I prayed he was almost out of his strongest spells. How many could he fit in those pockets?

The sun blazed bright on him, lighting his face up with a red glow that made him look like the devil. In fairness, the goatee didn't help matters.

"You two are more trouble than you're worth," he hissed.

I edged behind Ana's shield, powering up my sonic boom.

He hurled another vial to the ground. This time, an ice monster burst forth, eight feet tall if it was an inch. It gleamed in the light of the rising sun. Ricketts waved his arm, and the beast thundered toward us.

Ana charged up her shield, her magic swelling on the air. The luminescent barrier grew, but the ice monster kept coming.

My heart thundered. I drew my sword and shield from the ether, ready to take on the ice monster if I had to. But these things were strong.

Please work, I begged Ana's shield.

The beast roared as it neared, mouth opening to reveal long fangs made of ice, then slammed into the shield, breaking into a thousand pieces.

As Ricketts stared in shock, I dove low under the barrier and hurled my sonic boom at him. It burst through the air and bowled him over.

I sprinted for him, sword drawn, and leapt onto his prone form, straddling him. Before I could get my blade to his throat, he bucked, throwing me off.

Suddenly, he had a dagger in his hand. He lunged for me, slicing at my side.

Pain seared. Panic rose.

I kicked him in the stomach.

He gasped, rolling away from me, but I scrambled after him. He was climbing to his feet. If he had a transport charm, he'd get away!

But Ana was there, kicking him hard in the shoulder. Right where my first dagger had landed. He howled and flew backward.

I leapt onto him, lining my blade up with his throat, the point of my long sword pressed to his skin.

His eyes fluttered open.

"Why do you want our blood?" I demanded.

"Because of what you are."

"What are we?" I pressed the blade deeper against his throat. Blood trickled down his neck.

He grimaced. "You don't know?"

"Tell me!"

He chuckled, a pained expression on his face. "Oh, this is rich. She'll get a kick out of this."

"Who? Who is *she*?" I pressed the blade slightly deeper, enough to threaten. "And *what* are we?!"

A shadow cut out the rising sun. With my peripheral vision, I caught sight of Ana, Cade, Caro, and Ali walking toward us across the top of the pyramid. More of the Protectorate followed.

Backup.

A few moments later, they stopped, circling us.

Ricketts's eyes darted around to the rest of the group. A wild kind of fear, then determination, filled his eyes. "I'm dead anyway. She'll kill me for failing."

What the—?

He thrust himself up toward the sword, forcing the blade to pierce his throat.

Arterial blood sprayed me.

"Damn it!" I rolled off of him, gagging.

He choked on his blood, then lay still, dead eyes staring toward the sky.

I collapsed onto my butt, chest heaving. He'd killed himself. The bastard had killed himself rather than reveal what we were.

Cade nudged him with his toe. "Smart man."

Caro nodded. "Son of a demon didn't want to give up his information."

"Probably thought we'd torture it out of him," Ali said.

I looked up, disappointment and anger filling me. "Would you?"

They all shrugged.

"Not likely. But possible," Jude said. "Depends on what's at stake. How evil he is."

Ana stepped forward, pressing a wadded-up cloth to her bleeding shoulder. She kicked Ricketts in the ribs, then spit on him.

Then she met my gaze. "Let's get out of here."

CHAPTER THIRTEEN

Emily transported us back to the Protectorate in groups. Ana and I went last, along with Cade and Ricketts's body. I didn't know what they were going to do with him, and I didn't ask.

But then again, leaving bodies on top of archaeological sites was some pretty weird littering, so maybe they were just cleaning up.

It was still dark when we arrived, the early morning hours cold and silent. As soon as we appeared on the lawn in front of the castle, Caro and Haris hurried over to us.

"Come on," Caro said. "We'll head to the infirmary to get patched up, then it's eating time."

Since I ached all over, that sounded like a good idea. Food wouldn't be too bad, either.

"There's a procedure to these things!" Haris said. "You can't forget the beer, Caro. That's step three of celebrating a victory."

"Fine, fine!" She grinned. "Procedure is everything."

I looked over at Ana, suddenly at a loss.

We'd done our job—catching Ricketts—and they'd done theirs —providing backup and getting us our buggy back—so we should be leaving now.

But I was unsure.

And it was obvious from her expression that Ana was too.

I didn't want to like it here... Or to need to be here. But we did. We had nowhere to go, and it was possible that our concealment charms were gone, now that Ricketts was dead.

And this place was actually pretty awesome. It was hard not to like.

I glanced over at Cade, who stood only a few feet away. The idea of leaving him made my chest ache. Which was also pretty annoying, really.

"Stay," he said. "I think someone will want to talk to you in a little while. You'll want to hear what they have to say."

"Who?" I asked.

He just shook his head. "I'd tell you if I could."

"But then you'd have to kill me?"

He sighed dramatically. "Rules are rules."

A tiny chuckle tried to escape me.

"Come on," Caro said. "Eating time."

"Hang on!" Jude walked toward us and stopped in front of Ana and me. She looked at us both. "You did well, you two. Most initiates don't have the training or skills that you two have. But your time in Death Valley taught you well."

"Well, it was that or die," Ana said.

I grinned. But Jude's words warmed me.

"Whatever it was, I hope you'll consider the Paranormal Investigative Team when you complete your training."

"Oooh." Caro's brows rose. "What an honor."

"Thank you." I nodded at Jude. "I appreciate it."

I still didn't know if we were staying, but it was nice to be invited. To be wanted.

~

After getting patched up and eating a meal in the Great Hall with everyone, I was ready for a nap. Not that I knew where I'd take that nap—in the temporary room we'd been given?—but it didn't matter in the end.

Cade came and found Ana and me. He'd eaten on the other side of the hall, away from us, but I hadn't been able to keep my eyes off him.

Ana said he hadn't been able to keep his off me, either. His timing must have been impeccable, however, because I'd never noticed him looking.

"Will you two come with me?" he asked. "There's someone who would like to meet you."

"Someone new?"

He nodded.

I looked at Ana. We both shrugged, then rose and followed him out of the raucous Great Hall and toward the same room that had pulsed with power yesterday. The one that felt like strength and power.

As we neared, the feeling of magic grew stronger—even more so than yesterday. It was like the push and pull of massive waves.

I gasped, reaching for Ana's hand. She gripped mine hard, clearly feeling weird as well.

I looked at Cade. He looked totally unaffected.

"What is that?" Ana asked.

"I'll let her introduce herself." Cade stopped at the door.

Her? Magic of this strength was coming from a person? Wow.

He knocked, then pushed it open. The magic that rolled out nearly sent me to my knees. Cade gestured for us to enter.

I sucked in a deep breath and walked in on shaky legs. Ana followed, entering a room that was full of brilliantly colored paintings on the tall walls.

The door shut behind us. I could feel that Cade wasn't in the room, but all my attention was on the figure in front of us.

If it was a woman, then she was unlike any I'd ever seen.

She gleamed with a pale white light, her features almost

reptilian. When she stood, her form shimmered, as if she weren't really there at all. Almost like she was a ghost.

"Welcome, Bree and Ana." Her voice resonated with power, though it wasn't loud.

"Um, thank you." I shot Ana a quick glance, then approached the table. "But who are you?"

She gestured to the chairs in front of us. I eyed her warily as we sat.

She followed. "I'm Arach. The spirit of the dragon who gave her magic to create this castle."

"Dragon spirit." Holy crap. I'd never met a freaking dragon before. They were at the top of the paranormal pecking order. "The Protectorate was formed by dragons?"

"Yes. Before the Order of the Magica and the Shifter Council formed as the governments of the magical world, supernaturals needed someone to protect them. To help those in need when an injustice was done. So the dragons stepped in. Before they went for their long slumber, the dragons gave a small part of their magic to the Undercover Protectorate. It was their gift to the world. I volunteered to create the castle and be the spirit that would oversee operations, to the best of my ability."

"Holy crap," Ana breathed. "The Protectorate is cooler than I thought. There are dragons here."

Arach gave a small smile. "I am not able to stay here for long, however. It is difficult to control my corporeal form."

"But you came to meet us." What the heck was going on?

"Yes. You are special, Bree and Ana. There is something very unique about you. I thought so from the moment I learned of you, but these last few days have proven that to be true."

"Cade told you about my magic?" *Jerk.* I'd wondered if he'd blown my secret. I didn't know what that crazy water power was —but I certainly didn't want anyone else knowing about it.

"No," Arach said. "He has not spoken of you at all. Your mother told me about you."

"My mother?" Ana and I spoke in unison.

"How?" I demanded.

"She wrote us a letter just before she died, wanting to bring you here. Because of what you are, and the risks that the outside world poses to Unknowns such as yourselves."

I stiffened. Ana did as well.

"Don't worry." Arach held up her hands in a placating gesture. "We don't feel the same way as the Order of the Magica. Unknowns are safe here. Valued."

My muscles relaxed, but only slightly. The Order was famous for persecuting those who were different and powerful. Unknowns were both.

"How can we trust you?"

"You wear the Mark of Power," Arach said. "The four-pointed star mark at the top of your spine."

Shock dropped my stomach to my feet. I glanced at Ana. Only our mother knew that we had those marks.

Our mother had truly believed that revealing our species would get us killed. Yet she'd told Arach. She'd *trusted* Arach.

"If she sent you a letter before she died, why did it take you so long to find us?" Ana asked. "That was ten years ago."

"After she died, you ran immediately. When we went to the homestead in Alaska, you were gone. We finally found you about a year ago. Then we watched, waiting to see if you were worthy. That you were who your mother said you were. But when we realized that you were being harassed by Ricketts's men, we sent Cade and his fighters."

Good timing. "Did you determine that we are who our mother claimed?"

"You are. When your magic became unreliable, Bree, we knew that the change was coming. And I can feel that you have more magic now. Another power?"

I hesitated, but only briefly. Arach was no con-dragon. "I can control water now. It just happened. But I don't know why."

Ana shot me a *WTF?* glance.

Arach smiled. "You will be powerful. But you *must* learn to control your magic. Else it will devour you. Body. Mind."

"Devour?" Ana's voice quavered. My insides did the same.

"Yes. Unknowns have great magic that manifests later in life. Bree, you are going through that change now. If you can learn to control it, your true species will be revealed. If you cannot...you will stay an Unknown. A dead Unknown, because your power devoured you from the inside out. Like a dying star. Though the process may not be quick. It is different for everyone."

Shit.

I'd know about the changes coming—not about the potential *dying.* "Can you help me learn to control my magic?"

She nodded. "We are your best hope. You will have to train hard. And you, as well, Ana. Not just for your own benefit, but so that you can one day join one of our divisions. It is a great honor, but you must prove yourselves worthy."

I glanced at Ana, my head reeling.

"How many Unknowns are there?" I asked.

"In the last hundred years? Just you two." Her expression sobered. "Three, if you count your sister."

My heart leapt at the mention.

"Do you know where she is?" Ana demanded.

"Is she alive?" I asked.

"I do not know," Arach said.

"Would you help us find her?" I asked. *That* would be huge.

Arach hesitated a moment, then nodded. "Yes. You must focus on mastering your power. That takes precedence. But we will help."

That was fine. I didn't want to collapse in on myself like a dying star, so I was happy to make the deal. But that didn't mean I couldn't keep negotiating.

"How's the pay?" I asked.

"Quite good, depending on which division you join. Not what

you used to earn in Death Valley, but you wouldn't need as much. We'll take care of concealment charms, if the one that Ricketts gave you has faded with his death. It is vital that you continue to hide what you are from the outside world."

"Our mother's prophecy is true?"

"Yes. Someone will seek to use you—even kill you—for what you are."

Not great.

"But not you?" Ana asked.

I wanted to fist bump her, because that was a damned good question.

A small smile creased Arach's face. "I hope that it will be mutual. We will help you master your powers, and in return, you will work for one of our divisions, helping to protect the magical world."

"We've never worked for anyone else," I said. "I don't really want to. And frankly, I don't think I'd be any good at it."

"Once you're trained—which I imagine you won't like, as you will have to take orders—you will be on your own. Most jobs are self-driven here. You do it as you see fit. We're built on trust."

Trust. Just as Cade had said.

"Don't forget that you could have friends here. Security. A life." Arach's eyes seemed endlessly knowledgeable at this moment. Like she knew what we lacked.

She did. Because this was sounding tempting.

I looked at Ana, who gave a tiny nod.

I met Arach's gaze. "A trial period. Two months."

Arach smiled and nodded. "Excellent. I am glad to hear it."

Happiness burst inside me. I might be conflicted about working for someone else, but I'd really wanted to stay. At least for now. I don't think I'd realized how much.

A quiet knock sounded on the door.

"Perfect timing." Arach rose, and drifted toward the door. We stood and followed her.

"So, you really built this place?" I asked.

"Yes. The magic was a gift from the other dragons, before they went for their slumber. But this place is built from my blood and bones, and now my spirit guides it."

"Wow. That's a serious gift," Ana said.

Arach smiled and opened the door to reveal Caro. "Caro here will show you to your new apartment. Remember—train hard, and be worthy."

Caro waved to Arach. I turned to say goodbye, but the dragon spirit had disappeared into the air. Immediately, the immense magic that had filled the room faded a bit.

Caro bounced impatiently from foot to foot. Her platinum hair was in wild disarray and excitement gleamed in her steely eyes. For someone with such a terrifying and deadly magical gift —not to mention a stone-cold attitude in battle—she was much more chipper and lighthearted than I'd expected.

"So, what'd you think?" she asked, her brows wiggling. "You got to meet Arach! She normally *never* comes to see new members."

"Yeah, that was wild," I said.

"I had no idea that the Protectorate was *this* cool," Ana said.

"It is." Caro's face sobered a bit. "But she means it. You really do have to train hard and be worthy. It's our motto, and boy, do they mean it."

We had excellent motivation to try, at least.

"Since you're staying, let me show you to your new apartments!"

I glanced at Ana, intrigued. "All right."

Caro led us up the great stairs and through a maze of hallways of all styles—some done with silk wallpaper and chandeliers, others still in their original castle form, complete with flickering wall sconces. At one point, the Pugs of Destruction raced by, each carrying a large ham in its mouth. The last one—the winged pug —farted as it ran by.

"Watch out for them," Caro said. "They'll steal the beer right out of your hand."

As we neared the back of the castle, mullioned glass windows provided a view of the grass lawn and an ancient stone circle.

Cool.

As a girl who'd lived in shitty wooden houses in the middle of nowhere her whole life, it was pretty danged awesome.

Caro stopped in front of a wooden door painted deep blue. "This one's for you, Bree. Ana, yours is the one next to it." She pointed to a door about twenty meters down. "Come on. I'll show you up."

We followed her up the spiral staircase. The space was empty for the first thirty feet, with glowing yellow lights dotting the walls, and we only reached an actual room near the top. Caro pushed open a door to reveal a round living space.

I stepped in, my heart fluttering in my chest. I hated myself for it, but I honestly felt like a kid on Christmas morning.

The space was round, with a beautiful living room on one side and a kitchen on the other. *Gorgeous.* Until now, all we'd had was shitty hand-me-down furniture that had been crap fifty years ago.

This was so perfect, and so pretty, that I could hardly believe it.

"It's amazing," Ana said.

"No, *this* is amazing." Caro strolled toward one of the windows on the wall and waved us forward.

I followed, my head buzzing slightly. When I caught sight of the sweeping view of the cliffs and ocean at the back of the castle, I gasped. The stone circle sat right below my window.

"See?" Caro said. "Nice, right? Each tower is enchanted to look the way the inhabitant wants it to." She spun around, gesturing to the decor. "Apparently you like the modern contrasted with the historic. Very nice, if I do say so. Mine looks like a pixie unicorn vomited rainbows all over it."

"I wouldn't peg you as the type," Ana said.

Caro shrugged. "We like what we like."

If someone had asked me what my design aesthetic was, I'd have said something like "not broken." Apparently, this tower knew me better than I knew myself.

"This is insane." The luxury of this place boggled my mind. "Are you freaking serious? They let you live here?"

"Why not?" She shrugged. "People give up a lot to work and live here." She hesitated. "Well, honestly, most of us are losers and loners, so this is an upgrade. But still, there's nothing wrong with living in a nice place. It helps with recruitment."

"I'll say." Ana roamed toward the spiral iron staircase that led upstairs, presumably to a bedroom.

"Well, I'll leave you guys to it," Caro said. "You know which door is yours, Ana."

"Thank you," I said.

"No problem. I'm glad you're here!"

She hurried out of the room and down the stairs. Ana and I were silent until we heard the bottom door slam.

Then we turned to each other. I wanted to go check out her apartment, but the elephant in the room was about to trample me.

"Can you believe we're doing this?" I was still kind of shocked. We were survivors. Together, we could handle anything. We'd made it on our own all this time. But now, maybe we didn't have to?

"I can't believe it. No, I can." Ana shook her head. "It's a game changer. This place is amazing. And the *Undercover Protectorate.* That's really cool. Being a part of something like that."

"*If* we pass the training." I wanted to. I wanted to get ahold of my magic. And if this was as cool as it seemed, I wanted a place here. "Having a purpose other than survival would be...awesome."

We could help people who were as scared as we'd been. *As we were.* Because the threat wasn't over yet.

"Let's focus on the survival part, first," Ana said.

"I'm worried about what Ricketts said before he died."

"About the woman." Ana nodded. "I think you're right. He wasn't acting on his own at the end there. Someone had gotten to him. He didn't want money anymore—just my blood for some kind of ritual."

"We need to find out who." Not knowing was an axe hanging over my neck. "But at least now we have some help."

"And help finding Rowan." Ana spun in a circle, taking in the amazing view from all windows. "Rowan would love this."

Tears pricked my eyes. Rowan was the only thing that could make me cry. "She would."

"We'll find her." Ana swallowed hard. "If she's alive, we'll find her."

I reached for Ana's hand, squeezing tight. "I love you, nerd."

"Love you back, double-nerd."

I grinned. "Let's go check out your room."

"Yeah."

We walked out of my apartment and down the stairs, both quiet. Thinking.

Whatever came at us, we would figure it out. Together.

EPILOGUE

The day after we moved into our new apartments, Cade and I returned to Venice to help Squido clear out the remnants of Ricketts's underground lair so his family could return. A crew from the Protectorate hauled off the stuff that Hedy might want to check out, and the Order of the Magica had agreed to make this a protected area for the Italian Kappis. All in all, a win.

After we finished, Cade and I sat on the steps of San Zaccaria, catching our breath from the work and watching the sun set in a brilliant display of orange and pink.

"I think you'll do well at the Protectorate," Cade said.

"Thanks." We watched the sunset in silence for a while before I spoke. "Why didn't you tell anybody about my new power?"

Arach knew. And everyone else would eventually, as my powers manifested. But he hadn't spoken of it to anyone.

"It's not my story to tell."

I smiled, liking that answer. A cool breeze rustled over my face, smelling of flowers and night and happiness. The last one was weird, but I swore it was true.

The colors had faded from the sky and Cade stood, reaching down for my hand to help pull me up.

I took it, his large palm swallowing my own, the strength in his touch sending a frisson of pleasure zinging up my arm. I let him help me to my feet, my mind buzzing with awareness.

He stood so close that the scent of his skin wrapped around me, bringing with it the smell of a storm at sea. It soaked into me, making my head spin. Heat seared, warm and fierce, sinking into my muscles and sending electricity blazing through me.

I licked my lips, so intensely aware of him that it felt like we were one, and glanced up.

His gaze was on my face, heat in his green eyes. Tension pulled at his jaw, as if he were resisting.

What? Me?

His full lips parted, just slightly.

He wanted to kiss me.

With all the stress of the past few days—the past few years— riding on my back, all I wanted to do was forget. To do something fun and spontaneous and totally free.

I wanted Cade. And he wanted me. The heat that burned me came directly from him. From the grip of his strong hand that still cradled my own, a point of contact that seared me.

I threw my arms around Cade's neck and kissed him.

Once, hard on the mouth.

His lips were full and soft, giving me a buzz unlike any I'd ever experienced. It spun through my head and veins, lighting me up like a live wire. He groaned, low in his throat, and his hand tightened on mine.

I pulled away, panting.

He swallowed hard, gaze hot. There was desire, but also something else in his eyes. He swallowed again, regret flashing across his face.

"That can't happen again." His voice was rough.

Shit. "You didn't like it?"

"I wanted it. But you're a trainee with the Protectorate now," he said. "It's...a conflict of interest."

So he did like it!

But then my face flamed. I'd just made an ass of myself. And he was right. It *was* a conflict of interest. I wanted a place at the Protectorate—or at least to earn the right to be there and find Rowan, even if we didn't stay forever.

So making out with Cade was a terrible freaking idea. Not to mention the whole trust thing. Growing close to Cade was a one-way ticket to a giant mess.

I stepped back, nodding. "You're totally right. Bad idea. Very bad idea. Sorry. I should have asked before I kissed you."

"Don't be sorry. I should have said no, but I didn't want to." His voice was low. Warm.

Oh, hell. I stepped back a foot.

My new life was confusing enough. New home, new job, new threat to my life. But then he had to go and say something like that? Something that made it so clear that he actually *did* want me?

"Ready to go?" My voice squeaked. *Awkward.*

"Aye." His lips quirked up in a devastating smile.

We turned and walked away from the church, headed to the boat waiting in the canal. As we silently crossed the square, tension thrummed between us like a living thing.

Oh my fates. With this between us, it was going to be damned hard to work with him in the future. Whatever the future might bring.

THANK YOU FOR READING!

I hope you enjoyed Bree's first book as much as I enjoyed writing it. Reviews are *so* helpful to authors. I really appreciate all reviews, both positive and negative. If you want to leave one, you can do so on Amazon or GoodReads.

Join my mailing list at www.linseyhall.com/subscribe to stay updated. You'll also get a free ebook copy of *Hidden Magic*, the story of the FireSouls early adventures. Turn the page for an excerpt of *Hidden Magic*.

EXCERPT OF HIDDEN MAGIC

Jungle, Southeast Asia
  Five years before the events in Ancient Magic

"How much are we being paid for this job again?" I glanced at the dudes filling the bar. It was a motley crowd of supernaturals, many of whom looked shifty as hell.

"Not nearly enough for one as dangerous as this." Del frowned at the man across the bar, who was giving her his best sexy face. There was a lot of eyebrow movement happening. "Is he having a seizure?"

"Looks like it." Nix grinned. "Though I gotta say, I wasn't expecting this. We're basically in a tree, for magic's sake. In the middle of the jungle! Where are all these dudes coming from?"

"According to my info, there's a mining operation near here. Though I'd say we're more *under* a tree than *in* a tree."

"I'm with Cass," Del said. "Under, not in."

"Fair enough," Nix said.

We were deep in Southeast Asia, in a bar that had long ago been reclaimed by the jungle. A massive fig tree had grown over and around the ancient building, its huge roots strangling the stone walls. It was straight out of a fairy tale.

Monks had once lived here, but a few supernaturals of indeterminate species had gotten ahold of it and turned it into a watering hole for the local supernaturals. We were meeting our contact here, but he was late.

"Hey, pretty lady." A smarmy voice sounded from my left. "What are you?"

I turned to face the guy who was giving me the up and down, his gaze roving from my tank top to my shorts. He wasn't Clarence, our local contact. And if he meant "what kind of supernatural are you?" I sure as hell wouldn't be answering. That could get me killed.

"Not interested is what I am," I said.

"Aww, that's no way to treat a guy." He grabbed my hip, rubbed his thumb up and down.

I smacked his hand away, tempted to throat-punch him. It was my favorite move, but I didn't want to start a fight before Clarence got here. Didn't want to piss off our boss.

The man raised his hands. "Hey, hey. No need to get feisty. You three sisters?"

I glanced at Nix and Del, at their dark hair that was so different from my red. We were all about twenty, but we looked nothing alike. And while we might call ourselves sisters—*deirfiúr* in our native Irish—this idiot didn't know that.

"Go away." I had no patience for dirt bags who touched me without asking. "Run along and flirt with your hand, because that's all the action you'll be getting tonight."

His face turned a mottled red, and he raised a fist. His magic welled, the scent of rotten fruit overwhelming.

He thought he was going to smack me? Or use his magic against me?

Ha.

I lashed out, punching him in the throat. His eyes bulged and he gagged. I kneed him in the crotch, grinning when he keeled over.

"Hey!" A burly man with a beard lunged for us, his buddy beside him following. "That's no way—"

"To treat a guy?" I finished for him as I kicked out at him. My tall, heavy boots collided with his chest, sending him flying backward. I never used my magic—didn't want to go to jail and didn't want to blow things up—but I sure as hell could fight.

His friend raised his hand and sent a blast of wind at us. It threw me backward, sending me skidding across the floor.

By the time I'd scrambled to my feet, a brawl had broken out in the bar. Fists flew left and right, with a bit of magic thrown in. Nothing bad enough to ruin the bar, like jets of flame, because no one wanted to destroy the only watering hole for a hundred miles, but enough that it lit up the air with varying magical signatures.

Nix conjured a baseball bat and swung it at a burly guy who charged her, while Del teleported behind a horned demon and smashed a chair over his head. I'd always been jealous of Del's ability to sneak up on people like that.

All in all, it was turning into a good evening. A fight between supernaturals was fun.

"Enough!" the bartender bellowed. "Or no more beer!"

The patrons quieted immediately. Fights might be fun, but they weren't worth losing beer over.

I glared at the jerk who'd started it. There was no way I'd take the blame, even though I'd thrown the first punch. He should have known better.

The bartender gave me a look and I shrugged, hiking a thumb at the jerk who'd touched me. "He shoulda kept his hands to himself."

"Fair enough," the bartender said.

I nodded and turned to find Nix and Del. They'd grabbed our

beers and were putting them on a table in the corner. I went to join them.

We were a team. Sisters by choice, ever since we'd woken in a field at fifteen with no memories other than those that said we were FireSouls on the run from someone who had hurt us. Who was hunting us.

Our biggest goal, even bigger than getting out from under our current boss's thumb, was to save enough money to buy conceal-ment charms that would hide us from the monster who hunted us. He was just a shadowy memory, but it was enough to keep us running.

"Where is Clarence, anyway?" I pulled my damp tank top away from my sweaty skin. The jungle was damned hot. We couldn't break into the temple until Clarence gave us the infor-mation we needed to get past the guard at the front. And we didn't need to spend too much longer in this bar.

Del glanced at her watch, her blue eyes flashing with annoy-ance. "He's twenty minutes late. Old Man Bastard said he should be here at eight."

Old Man Bastard—OMB for short—was our boss. His name said it all. Del, Nix, and I were FireSouls, the most despised species of supernatural because we could steal other magical being's powers if we killed them. We'd never done that, of course, but OMB didn't care. He'd figured out our secret when we were too young to hide it effectively and had been blackmailing us to work for him ever since.

It'd been four years of finding and stealing treasure on his behalf. Treasure hunting was our other talent, a gift from the dragon with whom legend said we shared a soul. No one had seen a dragon in centuries, so I wasn't sure if the legend was even true, but dragons were covetous, so it made sense they had a knack for finding treasure.

"What are we after again?" Nix asked.

"A pair of obsidian daggers," Del said. "Nice ones."

"And how much is this job worth?" Nix repeated my earlier question. Money was always on our minds. It was our only chance at buying our freedom, but OMB didn't pay us enough for it to be feasible anytime soon. We kept meticulous track of our earnings and saved like misers anyway.

"A thousand each."

"Damn, that's pathetic." I slouched back in my chair and stared up at the ceiling, too bummed about our crappy pay to even be impressed by the stonework and vines above my head.

"Hey, pretty ladies." The oily voice made my skin crawl. We just couldn't get a break in here. I looked up to see Clarence, our contact.

Clarence was a tall man, slender as a vine, and had the slicked back hair and pencil-thin mustache of a 1940s movie star. Unfortunately, it didn't work on him. Probably because his stare was like a lizard's. He was more Gomez Addams than Clark Gable. I'd bet anything that he liked working for OMB.

"Hey, Clarence," I said. "Pull up a seat and tell us how to get into the temple."

Clarence slid into a chair, his movement eerily snakelike. I shivered and scooted my chair away, bumping into Del. The scent of her magic flared, a clean hit of fresh laundry, as she no doubt suppressed her instinct to transport away from Clarence. If I had her gift of teleportation, I'd have to repress it as well.

"How about a drink first?" Clarence said.

Del growled, but Nix interjected, her voice almost nice. She had the most self control out of the three of us. "No can do, Clarence. You know... Mr. Oribis"—her voice tripped on the name, probably because she wanted to call him OMB—"wants the daggers soon. Maybe next time, though."

"Next time." Clarence shook his head like he didn't believe her. He might be a snake, but he was a clever one. His chest puffed up a bit. "You know I'm the only one who knows how to get into the temple. How to get into any of the places in this jungle."

"And we're so grateful you're meeting with us. Mr. Oribis is so grateful." Nix dug into her pocket and pulled out the crumpled envelope that contained Clarence's pay. We'd counted it and found—unsurprisingly—that it was more than ours combined, even though all he had to do was chat with us for two minutes. I'd wanted to scream when I'd seen it.

Clarence's gaze snapped to the money. "All right, all right."

Apparently his need to be flattered went out the window when cash was in front of his face. Couldn't blame him, though. I was the same way.

"So, what are we up against?" I asked.

The temple containing the daggers had been built by supernaturals over a thousand years ago. Like other temples of its kind, it was magically protected. Clarence's intel would save us a ton of time and damage to the temple if we could get around the enchantments rather than breaking through them.

"Dvarapala. A big one."

"A gatekeeper?" I'd seen one of the giant, stone monster statues at another temple before.

"Yep." He nodded slowly. "Impossible to get through. The temple's as big as the Titanic—hidden from humans, of course—but no one's been inside in centuries, they say."

Hidden from humans was a given. They had no idea supernaturals existed, and we wanted to keep it that way.

"So how'd you figure out the way in?" Del asked. "And why *haven't* you gone in? Bet there's lots of stuff you could fence in there. Temples are usually full of treasure."

"A bit of pertinent research told me how to get in. And I'd rather sell the entrance information and save my hide. It won't be easy to get past the booby traps in there."

Hide? Snakeskin, more like. Though he had a point. I didn't think he'd last long trying to get through a temple on his own.

"So? Spill it," I said, anxious to get going.

He leaned in, and the overpowering scent of cologne and sweat hit me. I grimaced, held my breath, then leaned forward to hear his whispers.

～

As soon as Clarence walked away, the communications charms around my neck vibrated. I jumped, then groaned. Only one person had access to this charm.

I shoved the small package Clarence had given me into my short's pocket and pressed my fingertips to the comms charm, igniting its magic.

"Hello, Mr. Oribis." I swallowed my bile at having to be polite.

"Girls," he grumbled.

Nix made a gagging face. We hated when he called us girls.

"Change of plans. You need to go to the temple tonight."

"What? But it's dark. We're going tomorrow." He never changed the plans on us. This was weird.

"I need the daggers sooner. Go tonight."

My mind raced. "The jungle is more dangerous in the dark. We'll do it if you pay us more."

"Twice the usual," Del said.

A tinny laugh echoed from the charm. "Pay *you* more? You're lucky I pay you at all."

I gritted my teeth and said, "But we've been working for you for four years without a raise."

"And you'll be working for me for four more years. And four after that. And four after that." Annoyance lurked in his tone. So did his low opinion of us.

Del's and Nix's brows crinkled in distress. We'd always suspected that OMB wasn't planning to let us buy our freedom, but he'd dangled that carrot in front of us. What he'd just said made that seem like a big fat lie, though. One we could add to the many others he'd told us.

An urge to rebel, to stand up to the bully who controlled our lives, seethed in my chest.

"No," I said. "You treat us like crap, and I'm sick of it. Pay us fairly."

"I treat you like *crap,* as you so eloquently put it, because that is exactly what you are. *FireSouls."* He spit the last word, imbuing it with so much venom I thought it might poison me.

I flinched, frantically glancing around to see if anyone in the bar had heard what he'd called us. Fortunately, they were all distracted. That didn't stop my heart from thundering in my ears as rage replaced the fear. I opened my mouth to shout at him, but snapped it shut. I was too afraid of pissing him off.

"Get it by dawn," he barked. "Or I'm turning one of you in to the Order of the Magica. Prison will be the least of your worries. They might just execute you."

I gasped. "You wouldn't." Our government hunted and imprisoned—or destroyed—FireSouls.

"Oh, I would. And I'd enjoy it. The three of you have been more trouble than you're worth. You're getting cocky, thinking you have a say in things like this. Get the daggers by dawn, or one of you ends up in the hands of the Order."

My skin chilled, and the floor felt like it had dropped out from under me. He was serious.

"Fine." I bit off the end of the word, barely keeping my voice from shaking. "We'll do it tonight. Del will transport them to you as soon as we have them."

"Excellent." Satisfaction rang in his tone, and my skin crawled. "Don't disappoint me, or you know what will happen."

The magic in the charm died. He'd broken the connection.

I collapsed back against the chair. In times like these, I wished I had it in me to kill. Sure, I offed demons when they came at me on our jobs, but that was easy because they didn't actually die. Killing their earthly bodies just sent them back to their hell.

But I couldn't kill another supernatural. Not even OMB. It might get us out of this lifetime of servitude, but I didn't have it in me. And what if I failed? I was too afraid of his rage—and the consequences—if I didn't succeed.

"Shit, shit, shit." Nix's green eyes were stark in her pale face. "He means it."

"Yeah." Del's voice shook. "We need to get those daggers."

"Now," I said.

"I wish I could just conjure a forgery," Nix said. "I really don't want to go out into the jungle tonight. Getting past the Dvarapala in the dark will suck."

Nix was a conjurer, able to create almost anything using just her magic. Massive or complex things, like airplanes or guns, were outside of her ability, but a couple of daggers wouldn't be hard.

Trouble was, they were a magical artifact, enchanted with the ability to return to whoever had thrown them. Like boomerangs. Though Nix could conjure the daggers, we couldn't enchant them.

"We need to go. We only have six hours until dawn." I grabbed my short swords from the table and stood, shoving them into the holsters strapped to my back.

A hush descended over the crowded bar.

I stiffened, but the sound of the staticky TV in the corner made me relax. They weren't interested in me. Just the news, which was probably being routed through a dozen techno-witches to get this far into the jungle.

The grave voice of the female reporter echoed through the quiet bar. "The FireSoul was apprehended outside of his apartment in Magic's Bend, Oregon. He is currently in the custody of the Order of the Magica, and his trial is scheduled for tomorrow morning. My sources report that execution is possible."

I stifled a crazed laugh. Perfect timing. Just what we needed to hear after OMB's threat. A reminder of what would happen if he turned us into the Order of the Magica. The hush that had descended over the previously rowdy crowd—the kind of hush you get at the scene of a big accident—indicated what an interesting freaking topic this was. FireSouls were the bogeymen. *I* was the bogeyman, even though I didn't use my powers. But as long as no one found out, we were safe.

My gaze darted to Del and Nix. They nodded toward the door. It was definitely time to go.

As the newscaster turned her report toward something more boring and the crowd got rowdy again, we threaded our way between the tiny tables and chairs.

I shoved the heavy wooden door open and sucked in a breath of sticky jungle air, relieved to be out of the bar. Night creatures screeched, and moonlight filtered through the trees above. The jungle would be a nice place if it weren't full of things that wanted to kill us.

"We're never escaping him, are we?" Nix said softly.

"We will." Somehow. Someday. "Let's just deal with this for now."

We found our motorcycles, which were parked in the lot with a dozen other identical ones. They were hulking beasts with massive, all-terrain tires meant for the jungle floor. We'd done a lot of work in Southeast Asia this year, and these were our favored forms of transportation in this part of the world.

Del could transport us, but it was better if she saved her power. It wasn't infinite, though it did regenerate. But we'd learned a long time ago to save Del's power for our escape. Nothing worse than being trapped in a temple with pissed off guardians and a few tripped booby traps.

We'd scouted out the location of the temple earlier that day, so we knew where to go.

I swung my leg over Secretariat—I liked to name my vehicles

—and kicked the clutch. The engine roared to life. Nix and Del followed, and we peeled out of the lot, leaving the dingy yellow light of the bar behind.

Our headlights illuminated the dirt road as we sped through the night. Huge fig trees dotted the path on either side, their twisted trunks and roots forming an eerie corridor. Elephant-ear sized leaves swayed in the wind, a dark emerald that gleamed in the light.

Jungle animals howled, and enormous lightning bugs flitted along the path. They were too big to be regular bugs, so they were most likely some kind of fairy, but I wasn't going to stop to investigate. There were dangerous creatures in the jungle at night —one of the reasons we hadn't wanted to go now—and in our world, fairies could be considered dangerous.

Especially if you called them lightning bugs.

A roar sounded in the distance, echoing through the jungle and making the leaves rustle on either side as small animals scurried for safety.

The roar came again, only closer.

Then another, and another.

"Oh shit," I muttered. This was bad.

~~~

Join my mailing list to get a free copy of *Hidden Magic.* No spam and you can leave anytime!

AUTHOR'S NOTE

Thanks for reading *Undercover Magic!* If you've read any of my previous books, you may have noticed that I have a fondness for including historical places and mythological elements. I did the same with *Undercover Magic*. Sometimes the history of these things is so interesting that I want to share more, so I like to do it in the Author's Note instead of the story itself.

On of the biggest historical elements of the book is Cade—otherwise known as Belatucadros, the Celtic god of war. The Celts were not actually a single kingdom or religion—rather, they were a people who shared cultural similarities during the Iron Age. Between 800 BC and 500 AD, they lived in a vast territory stretching from Ireland all the way to Eastern Europe and down into Spain, Portugal, and parts of Italy. Though we think of Celtic as being traditionally Irish and Scottish, it originated in what is now Austria. Celtic culture then spread outward, covering most of Europe. Because of the Roman Conquest, Ireland and the British Isles were the last places to have Celtic-speaking communities (all the way up to the 6th century AD), which is why we initially think of them when we hear the word *Celtic*.

Because of the massive spread of Celtic culture and the many different kinds of Celts, there were multiple Celtic gods of war. Belatucadros was worshiped in northern Britain around the time of the Roman Conquest at the beginning of the first millennium AD. Evidence of his existence (in the minds of the ancient Celts and Romans) exists from 28 inscriptions on Hadrian's Wall, which was built to keep the Romans from conquering what is now Scotland. Roman soldiers actually worshiped Belatucadros, who is associated with their war god, Mars. His name is often translated as 'fair slayer' or 'fair shining one'. So I suppose he was handsome, which works for Cade.

As for the rest of the history in *Undercover Magic*, the scene in Venice was really fun to write, because Venice is full of great historical places. Poveglia Island really is a plague quarantine island used in 1776 to house plague victims who came in on ships destined for Venice. There was an asylum for the mentally ill built on the island in the early 20th century, and the island is now mostly abandoned.

The Vampire of Venice is based on a body discovered on the plague island of Lazzaretto Nuovo, which is located close to Poveglia Island. The skeleton of a woman was dated to the Venetian plague of 1576 and was found with a brick jammed between her jaws. This was a medieval practice meant to prevent vampires from continuing to feed after they'd been put into the ground.

San Zaccaria is a real church in Venice with a flooded crypt. But even more interesting than that —the room of skulls and bones is based on a real place. It is based on the Capuchin Crypt in Rome (though there is a similar one in Paris). The Capuchin crypt is decorated with the skeletal remains of 3,700 bodies that are believed to be the Capuchin friars who served the order between 1528 and 1870.

The first bodies used to decorate the crypt in 1631 came from the friar's old monastery—they brought 300 wagons full of the bones of deceased friars. The new additions to the crypt were allowed to decompose for roughly 30 years in the soil before being exhumed and placed in the crypt. There are six rooms in the crypt—the Crypt of the Skulls, the Crypt of the Pelvises, the Crpyt of the Leg Bones and Thigh Bones, the Crypt of Three Skeletons, the Crypt of the Resurrection, and the Mass Chapel. This place is meant to be a reminder of our mortality and short time on earth.

The fist fight bridge that Cade and Bree drive under in their boat is based on Ponte dei Pugni, the Bridge of Fists. The tradition of fighting atop the bridge began in the early 17th century, and they were hugely popular. They were held in neighborhoods all over Venice (on more than one bridge) and the fighters were often sponsored by the wealthy elite. Four fighters would stand on the bridge—one in each corner—and fight to throw the others off into the water. The last remaining fighter won. In 1705, the fight devolved into a riot and they were outlawed for good.

As for some of the history in the rest of the book—Arach is Gaelic for dragon. The Bad Water is a real place in Death Valley —an ancient dried out salt lake—but I don't think there are any salt monsters there. The final scene at the Aztec city is based on Tenochtitlan, the Aztec capital (1321-1525 AD). It was once surrounded by a marshy lake, though it now is in the middle of Mexico city. The giant frog, called the Cueyatle, is one of their mythical beasts. And the winged snake that attacks Bree on pyramid is Quetzacoatle, a god who contributed to the creation of mankind. He was protecting the sacrifice, which hadn't happened there in a long time.

I mention that Cass, Del, and Nix are treasure hunters who return the artifact to its original resting place. They do this because its morally and legally the right thing to do, and I am an archaeologist as well as a writer, so it is important to me.

Well, I think that's it for the history and mythology in *Undercover Magic*. I hope you enjoyed the book and will come back for more of Bree, Ana, and Cade!

ACKNOWLEDGMENTS

Thank you, Ben, for everything. There would be no books without you.

Thank you to Jena O'Connor, Lindsey Loucks, and Donna Rich for your excellent editing. The book is immensely better because of you! Thank you to Eleonora for finding errors and improving the book! Thank you to Orina Kafe for the beautiful cover art. Thank you to Collette Markwardt for allowing me to borrow the Pugs of Destruction, who are real dogs named Chaos, Havoc, and Ruckus. They were all adopted from rescue agencies.

GLOSSARY

Alpha Council - There are two governments that enforce law for supernaturals—the Alpha Council and the Order of the Magica. The Alpha Council governs all shifters. They work cooperatively with the Alpha Council when necessary—for example, when capturing FireSouls.

Blood Sorcerer - A type of Magica who can create magic using blood.

Dark Magic - The kind that is meant to harm. It's not necessarily bad, but it often is.

Demons - Often employed to do evil. They live in various hells but can be released upon the earth if you know how to get to them and then get them out. If they are killed on Earth, they are sent back to their hell.

Dragon Sense - A FireSoul's ability to find treasure. It is an internal sense that pulls them toward what they seek. It is easiest to find gold, but they can find anything or anyone that is valued by someone.

Djinn - Possesses invisibility and the ability to possess others for brief periods of time.

Earthwalking Gods - Reincarnates of the ancient gods who can walk upon the earth. They are mortal but with all the power of that god.

Enchanted Artifacts – Artifacts can be imbued with magic that lasts after the death of the person who put the magic into the artifact (unlike a spell that has not been put into an artifact—these spells disappear after the Magica's death). But magic is not stable. After a period of time—hundreds or thousands of years depending on the circumstance—the magic will degrade. Eventually, it can go bad and cause many problems.

Fire Mage – A mage who can control fire.

FireSoul - A very rare type of Magica who shares a piece of the dragon's soul. They can locate treasure and steal the gifts (powers) of other supernaturals. With practice, they can manipulate the gifts they steal, becoming the strongest of that gift. They are despised and feared. If they are caught, they are thrown in the Prison of Magical Deviants.

The Great Peace - The most powerful piece of magic ever created. It hides magic from the eyes of humans.

Magica - Any supernatural who has the power to create magic —witches, sorcerers, mages. All are governed by the Order of the Magica.

Order of the Magica - There are two governments that enforce law for supernaturals—the Alpha Council and the Order of the Magica. The Order of the Magica govern all Magica. They work cooperatively with the Alpha Council when necessary—for example, when capturing FireSouls.

Seeker - A type of supernatural who can find things. FireSouls often pass off their dragon sense as Seeker power.

Shifter - A supernatural who can turn into an animal. All are governed by the Alpha Council.

Transporter - A type of supernatural who can travel anywhere. Their power is limited and must regenerate after each use.

Undercover Protectorate - A secret organization dedicated to protecting supernaturals and solving the crimes that no one else will.

Vampire - Blood drinking supernaturals with great strength and speed who live in a separate realm.

ABOUT LINSEY

Before becoming a writer, Linsey Hall was a nautical archaeologist who studied shipwrecks from Hawaii and the Yukon to the UK and the Mediterranean. She credits fantasy and historical romances with her love of history and her career as an archaeologist. After a decade of tromping around the globe in search of old bits of stuff that people left lying about, she settled down and started penning her own romance novels. Her Dragon's Gift series draws upon her love of history and the paranormal elements that she can't help but include.

COPYRIGHT

Made in the USA
Middletown, DE
29 July 2018